CONTENTS

Copyrights and Acknowledgements

We wish to express our thanks to the authors and literary agents for their permission to publish the stories in this volume.

Cover Artwork by Rosalie-Ann Modder
Cover Design by Andrew Duke

PREFACE

The first generation Nigerian Writers are well known and acknowledged. Writers of Nigerian descent have won accolades and awards all over the world. But while the same writers have dominated the landscape for upwards of half a century (save for a handful of recently published younger writers) the creative writing enterprise has almost died by reason of economic, political and socio-cultural problems. This condition is not helped by the lack of publishers' interest in these new writers. While new writers have continued to be proficient even in the face of economic and political hardship, publishers have continued to recycle the same writers and writings with such profligacy that readers may be tempted to believe that there are just a few writers worth publishing in Nigeria.

The intent of this work is to set the record straight and showcase the talents of yet to be acknowledged writers who have continued to produce outstanding works, undaunted by the prospect of not being published. It is sad to note that while preparing this publication, we lost one of the contributors whose major groundbreaking poetry collections are yet to be published. There is therefore an urgent need to get new talents and views published in their lifetimes. Posthumous awards are of no real use to a writer, are they?

For readers who are used to Nigerian writers, this collection is an opportunity to gain another insight into the diversity of writings that emanate from that country. In this compilation, there is a fresh take on culture, society and literature. This compilation presents a modern view of the existence of Nigerians in the last two to three decades. While the stories are modern, an expression of the exposure of our contributors (most of whom have travelled widely), they are also distinctly Nigerian; reflecting the changing culture, values, and thoughts. It is refreshing to see how the recent political and economic problems in Nigeria have affected the pattern and subject matter of some of the stories. In short, this is a celebration of the resiliency of Nigeria and Nigerians wherever they may be.

For readers who may be coming across Nigerian literature for the first time, we have presented in this compilation the authentic and original literary voice of a generation who have refused to be wasted despite the combined effects of; civil war, ethnic bigotry, civilian misadministration, military brigandage and the mindless neo-colonisation by foreign powers and the resultant effect of these on the collective psyche of Nigerians. You will find the subject matter in these stories as diverse and complex as the Nigerian State. And like the country, the stories are interesting and unique, and will usher you into a new understanding of the African art of storytelling.

I welcome you to this experience and I hope you will look forward to the next volume in our series.

Yinka Smart-Babalola
Publisher
June 99'

*This book is dedicated to the ever-living memory of
Kolapo Oyefeso, the great bard, who left
unannounced.*

LIVING IN THE LIGHT

By

Chukwuma Okoye-Nwajiaga

She had neither known nor imagined such malignant loneliness, fear, poverty and despair that had plagued her life for the past couple of years. As a young girl she had counted herself amongst the fortunate. She'd had averagely comfortable parents: a generous and gay father, and a dutiful mother whom she had lost at the age of twelve. She was in Class One then at Girl's Secondary School, Ihiala. Although her nostalgic memory trips revealed her mother as a somewhat maternal angel, she could not help holding her responsible for her state of ignorance, which in a way may have landed her in her present state of acute misery. There were things she needed to know: about the world, about men. But her parents were incurably Catholic and protected her devoutly from all knowledge of the corruption that is in the world; personified in that most incorrigible fiend – man. She could excuse her father now, fathers being what they are. He loved her and would easily have come to her rescue were he to be made aware of her present predicament. But certainly not her mother. There were things she should have told her, things she should have prepared her for. But no. Or perhaps she knew no better. Perhaps she too was reasonably ignorant and hid this behind her mask of affability.

No! The more she thought of her past the more intensely the present burns her skull, spilling droplets of piercing bright tears down her cheeks. Why are women this unlucky? She wondered. But are all women this unlucky? This forlorn and distressed? No! Her mother, for instance, was not. In her memory she was visibly happy and contented. Her every memory of her was of an exceedingly happy and caring woman. A woman who had a kind word and gesture for everyone. A woman who devoutly espoused one of Jesus Christ's most important injunctions to mankind: Love thy neighbour as thyself. The entire world was her neighbour. Even inside the coffin her mother had beamed with a most disquieting aliveness such that she was afraid to look her in the face. She had felt – this she remembered vividly – that she was alive and wide-awake. In fact, she could even discern a certain cynicism on her face as she lay there, watching everyone behind closed lids with benevolent aloofness.

For several days she was unable to erase the last image of her mother's face from her mind. Her memory was tortuously vivid and cynical. Perhaps that was the reason she felt towards her the way she did now. Somehow she read in that valedictory benevolent attitude an expression of sadistic pleasure. And she felt strongly that that attitude was specifically for her benefit. Perhaps she was telling her that she would never be as happy as she had been since she was returning with all knowledge of things of happiness. Thus she was the only one who did not shed a single tear as she was lowered into the grave and covered with earth. She was sad naturally, but the tears refused to fall. Even her father dispensed a few drops. But not her. She simply could not find them.

But sometimes Daku wondered whether her mother was truly what she appeared to be. Was she honestly happy – even in death? Or was her entire life filled with lies? She was almost unbearably cheery.

Even in her childish mind she'd often felt that her mother was not to be trusted. She had an uncanny feeling that she was holding something back from her and everyone.... But why did she always think of her mother whenever she was on the verge of a major decision? And why had she found it impossible to excise that valedictory expression on her mother's face from her being? She had been dead now for thirteen years, yet she had this malevolent presence in her mind. She must not think of her anymore. Especially in those terms. There was a traditionally prescribed statute forbidding harsh thoughts of the dead. The dead were ancestral beings, powerful and supernal. She wondered if her mother could see her now and what her feelings would be towards her in this mournful state. She could not help the feeling that her mother would be happy to see the ruins of her life lying scattered around her feet. And she had neither the strength nor the willingness to bend down now and pick herself up. Oh! How she wished she could eschew all these weird thoughts from her head. Thoughts of the dead had become her engaging fascination since she began to lose her mind. Or was she losing her mind? It had become so difficult for her to think of life. Once again she wondered how unfortunate she was to be a woman. And once again she wondered how her life had come to this.

She was one of the very privileged girls in her community who had the tenacity to complete their secondary school education. Very many got married and had to drop out. But her father was resolved on her finishing secondary school. So she did. She even went on to a Teacher Training College. She, however, could not finish. She spent only a year therein. She had to get married. Her father had grown tired of fending the relentless suitors off. So he'd finally consented. After all she had completed Secondary School and a year of Teacher Training. She was no longer illiterate. So she had to get married. At that time she was woefully ignorant of men and was exceedingly nervous in their presence. But she had to marry one of them. Of all the hounds that sought her hand – of these there were many for she was truly a very attractive young girl – she was fascinated by a certain young man called Dubu, perhaps because he was the only one who was well educated. At the time she was still in awe of education. And Dubu was a teacher in a certain distant college. He was also younger than most of the other suitors. In any case she could not specifically say why the lot fell on Dubu. But it did. So she married him.

Now whenever she remembered how happy she had been on her wedding day, sad tears trickled down her cheeks. Why was it impossible to continue being that happy? She actually thought she would. She thought she had entered a life of eternal bliss. So she entered Dubu's two-room apartment in the school compound with a skin laden with the joy of ignorance. But now in her husband's house she began to know, to discover life and all its unfair and unsavoury properties. She began to know people, and she began to know man.

She resisted his heated approaches every night for a week. Then she got tired-or fed up, or disgusted. She was made to understand that she could not stay him off forever. So she gave in.

The night he split her skin of ignorance she wept freely. Not from the pain, nor from the blood. She wept from the feeling of loneliness and filthiness that overwhelmed her. Especially after the erstwhile zealous Dubu finished and, as if he had no more use of her, turned his back on her and soon began to snore. She hated herself. She hated Dubu. She hated her father who gave her away. She hated the world. She hated man. But most of all she hated womanhood which was no more than a receptacle for the clammy scum that was man. Goose bumps sprouted all over her skin. She could not bear the murky sensation inside of her, so she kept her legs apart. Soon she was flooded with nausea. She ran out of the room in time to discharge the bitter bile that coursed through her into the toilet. And then she vigorously washed the scum from her private part. If only her mother had warned her. Perhaps her life wouldn't have come to this. She had become wasted even before she had started living. Since then she loathed Dubu's touch and hated this his business of plunging into her with disgusting fervour. So she searched for and discovered a way of keeping herself intact while Dubu struggled on top of her, moaning obscenely and gasping like a dog out of breath. He often complained of her frigidity and unwillingness. First he tried to bribe her with kindness and tenderness. When that failed he began to use her wickedly; riding and whipping her like a horse. But all that happened only to her body. Her self was removed, like an indifferent observer, to a distance beyond Dubu's loathsome passion. When he was through and she returned to herself she would begin to weep softly. By then Dubu would have turned his snoring head against the wall, oblivious to the world. She would move into the bathroom like a zombie and thoroughly wash out Dubu's stickiness.

Even in Dubu's house she could not describe herself as well fed. She discovered that teachers did not possess as much money as books. And Dubu's books were enormous and particularly inedible. Compared to the life she had lived in her father's house she was practically starving. Yet she never complained. She knew countless other women whose husbands apparently earned less money than hers, and other women who had children to feed. Some of who lived in one-room apartments. So she reasoned that perhaps she would soon get used to her new life of drudgery. Perhaps Dubu was purposely torturing her. For what? She even tried to cope with his vile touch. But it was no use. To that she was practically dead.

A concerned neighbour advised her to go into petty trading but Dubu would not hear of it. He would not have his wife selling garri and vegetables in the market, like the wife of some common illiterate hunter. She herself suggested sewing and mending clothes for the school children with the sewing machine, which was a wedding present from her father, but Dubu would not hear of it either. So she spent virtually all her life imprisoned in Dubu's two-room affair, every day except for Sundays.

She was never really as religious as she was brought up to be, but in Dubu's house she developed an overwhelming love for the Catholic mass. This was, however, for no religious reason. It provided her the only moments of freedom she had. She relished these masses. She enjoyed and worshipped these masses. She saw the whole world dressed in brilliant colours, smiling radiantly like stars in the nightlight. She saw people behave the way they should, like civilised beings. People went out of their way to be courteous and polite to each other - even to her. Although she was not deceived by this artificiality she enjoyed them and even tried herself to take an active part, to match everyone attitude for attitude. She wished the world never had to remove these Sunday masks. Even Dubu became somebody else during these masses. He would put his arm tenderly and fondly across her shoulders and introduce her to some of his friends. At these moments Dubu always sounded proud of her.

But she was not deceived. So she often wondered at the holiness of the Holy Communion, which they all partook of during these masses. Even Dubu.

The host looked really sacred, almost blindingly incandescent. When the priest held it tenderly and raised it up, she always saw two sharp bolts of light from the sky pierce through the stained glass of the two windows on each side of the altar and arrest the host in the priest's hands momentarily with a brilliant yellow halo as the little bell tore divinely into the silence. She really felt that these communions were truly holy. But how could something that holy bear to be swallowed so affectedly piously by these people whose bodies housed the most unholy of deeds, feelings, wishes, thoughts, desires; people whose insides were filled with all forms of extortion and iniquity. Even Dubu never failed to receive the communion on Sunday. So she wondered. Yet she never gave up the divine expectation that one day she would witness a most haunting truth; she would watch happily as these wicked ones who had brazenly gone on their knees and received the communion would burst violently, spewing their iniquities in jets, flooding the entire church building. As a matter of fact she had seen Dubu go to pieces over this Holy Communion. He was returning from the altar, his palms piously clasped before his chest. Then all of a sudden he bloated and burst with a violent retort. His wickedness gushed out and filled the entire church building. But amongst this wickedness glowed the brilliance of the little piece of host. It hung above him awhile and then slowly it began to ascend with all the light of the world, back to the one who once said, "let there be light". But in the transitory darkness that enveloped her vision she felt Dubu making to take his seat beside her. Then she wondered once again at the holiness of the Communion. But yet she was convinced it would happen one day. Soon. Every evil soul shall burst. And she would be there to count them.

It was on such a day, imprisoned, as she was in Dubu's bedroom, brooding over her woeful fate, that she saw him. By all means she must have dozed off. But she could swear she was wide-awake. Just before he entered an eerie chilly wind blew into the room, swelling the white curtains in a rhythmic billow. She felt cold within in spite of the hot weather. Her head swelled and she felt weightless, floating amongst the celestial bodies. Then he entered effortlessly - the old man with the benign expression. His head was almost completely bald but for the thin fringe of grey which ran round the base of his head from ear to ear. Daku was mesmerised, but somehow felt no fear. Her entire self had been arrested, awaiting redemption. Then he spoke in a most gentle and sonorous voice.

"Do not be afraid my daughter for I have seen your unhappiness and have come to help you", he told her. She made to get up but he motioned her to sit down. So she remained where she was, starring fearlessly but helplessly into the gentle face of this aged stranger.

"Do you know who I am?"

"No father", she replied.

"I know you don't. I am the father of the man to whom you are married. So in a way you are my daughter and I am your father"

"But you are dead father"

"Yes, but not to you my daughter. I can see you are very sad. That is why I have come to see you. Tell me what your problems are." Daku felt the floodgate of her sorrows fling violently open. She began hurriedly to let flow her sorrows and her imprisoned emotions. She told him everything.

"But I trained my son very well in school so how could he be poor?" he wondered.

"We are very poor father. My husband does not bring any money home and he won't let me make some money myself."

"He is wicked. He cannot claim to be poor. I made sure of that. I gave him education when it was very expensive. He is to use it on his wife and children, the very way I lavished my wealth on him. Yet he killed me..."

"What?" Shrieked Daku, in surprise.

"Do not worry about that. I shall think of a way to help you out of your sorrows."

"But father, don't you have any money at all to give me?" Daku implored.

"No. But don't worry. I shall find a way out. Yes..."

His voice echoed in the room as both sound and vision receded into nothingness. Then she began to shiver uncontrollably. She was still like that when Dubu came back from school. He was going to have a go at her about lunch when he saw the state she was in.

"What's the matter? Are you ill?" he enquired.

"No," Daku replied.

"Then what is it?" Dubu asked impatiently. So she told him. She could hold nothing back. She told him everything. Then Dubu flared up quite unreasonably at the end of her narration. He was unexpectedly furious, as if it had really happened, as if it was not a dream after all. Perhaps he knew it was not.

"Why did you tell him you were hungry?" he queried.

"I'm sorry. I don't know. I couldn't help it." Daku was afraid he would beat her again today.

"Foolish woman. And he promised to help did he not? We shall see. Coward." He began to pace the room furiously. "Coward!" he screamed at the walls. "Why didn't you come to me? It's very like you to go to a woman. Coward, come to me and I will kill you again." And he said I was wicked right?" he turned to Daku. She was too afraid to reply. She nodded her head timidly.

"And he said he lavished his wealth on me?" He asked again. Again Daku nodded.

"Liar!" he bellowed. Daku cringed with fear. "Liar! I say he is a bloody liar. You are a bloody liar!" he screamed at the walls. "But we shall see. You set your foot in my house again. Let you ...Oh."

Daku was surprised at the intensity of Dubu's anger. She was terrified for she had never really seen him this agitated. And worst of all she could not understand the reason for this outrage. The man who had appeared to her was dead. It obviously must have been a dream, some kind of vivid dream. But here was her husband getting thoroughly worked up over it. There was certainly something sinister, something unreal in this whole affair. Somehow she felt used in this battle – or whatever it was – between father and son. Again she felt like a receptacle, helpless. But how could he even tell that it was his father she saw in that dream. How could he? She was hopelessly confused and of a sudden it occurred to her that her mother must be happy being dead. It occurred to her that if she herself were dead she would be free of this misery. Then she began to long for death.

"Hopeless idiot! What did you leave behind?" raged Dubu insanely. "Yes what did he leave behind for me when he died? And he said I was wicked right?" he asked. Daku could bear it no longer. She began to cry profusely. Dubu stared at her with horrid insane flames in his eyes. "Both of you. All right I'll be back." He left the obvious threat unfinished and stormed out of the house, banging the door hard after him.

That afternoon Daku thought of packing her things and running away. But where could she run? She could run to her father, but where would she find the money to pay for the transportation? Apart from that she had begun to find solace in thoughts of death. She was fed up with life. Obviously her creation was an error, which could be corrected with her exit. Life in the world they said is a visitation, after which one ultimately returned to...wherever. As with visitations some last very long – especially when they are welcomed – while others only last a short while. She obviously belonged to the latter category. Hers was a short visit indeed. She was no longer welcome to stay. There was a divine hand in the whole affair and she could not help it. So she had to leave, to go back home, as it were. Even now she began to pray that her next visit should not be as steeped in misery as this – as if this first one were already over. This thought of death fluttered in her head as she smoothly and gratefully passed into sleep.

Daku dreamt she was dead and in the land of the dead. She saw her mother. Her mother was surprisingly happy to see her. In fact it seemed she had been long awaited. She asked after Dubu's father but her mother did not know him. She explained that the place was much more populated than the world of the living. She needed to see him so she searched among the multitude of faces. But she could not find him.

She was still searching when she felt herself being fondled. For the first time in her life she felt the pleasure of a man's touch. She was responding eagerly when she realised that she was no longer in the world of her mother. There was a strong acrid smell of alcohol close to her nose. She woke up and realised that it was Dubu at his disgusting business again. She froze, but this time her soul refused to leave her body. She was unable to put herself away from Dubu's lecherous reach. So she began to fight. She jerked her body aside and brought her knee up violently. Dubu screamed out obviously hit on a spot that registered much pain.

"You foolish woman, are you crazy?" he bellowed, his two hands clutching his crotch. Daku sprang up from the bed and made for the door, but Dubu recovered quickly and grabbed her before she could get there. He flung her violently back into the room. She fell on the bed and hit her head against the wall. Bright little stars sparkled in the darkness of her brain. Then Dubu began to thrash her mercilessly. But this time she did not cry out as usual. She could not. She was already going back home in her mind and nothing mattered to her much anymore. This whole visit was over and she was homeward bound. So she merely curled herself up into a tight ball and received all of Dubu's drunken blows. Soon he got tired and began to snore long before he collapsed on the bed on top of her. She pushed him aside, got up and moved into the parlour where she folded herself on the small couch. She could no longer bear to be close to him. She would be dead before she would ever let herself live in the same house with him again. But what could she do? She turned this over and over in her head until she felt the welcome embrace of sleep.

She woke up with a start almost immediately. She felt a certain presence in the darkness around her. But it was a benign presence. Her mind was surprisingly clear and pure. She felt elated, almost liberated. There was no more sadness; no more pain; no more anger, no more confusion. She was a different person now. Totally new. She got up from the couch, turned the light on and began to put the room in order.

Her movements were slow, detached and measured. First she went to the bathroom and washed herself particularly thoroughly. Then she put on her finest dress, which she had worn to the mass the previous Sunday. She took pains to make herself up in the mirror. She smiled at the beauty that seemed to spring at her from her reflection in the mirror. She was certainly a woman of uncommon beauty. She moved into the bedroom and turned on the light. Dubu was curled up on the bed deep in sleep. He had an innocent, peaceful expression on his face, the kind he usually wore from the altar, his palms put together before him and the holy host slowly dissolving in his mouth. Daku smiled distantly at this familiar mask, which incidentally was out of place. It was usually worn for the mass on Sunday. She walked measuredly into the kitchen where she picked up the long kitchen knife and the heavy pestle. With these she walked back into the bedroom. Dubu had turned in his sleep and now lay stretched out on his back, his arms lying demurely by his side. His chest seemed thrust out rather expectantly. He still wore that pious mask of the Sunday mass. Daku knelt down by the bed, genuflected and raised the knife up above Dubu's chest. All of a sudden the familiar bolts of light broke through the windows and framed the tip of the knife in that brilliant yellow halo. When the little bell stopped ringing she turned the knife upside down and placed the tip lightly on Dubu's chest, in the position of his heart. As soon as the knife touched his chest the radiant halo spread all over his body, framing his entire body now as it did the tip of the knife. She raised the pestle high over her head and tightened the grip on the handle of the knife in her left hand. With all her strength she struck the protruding end of the handle with the heavy pestle. It passed smoothly and eagerly through his chest;

through his heart; through the bed sheet; and buried its tip in the old Vita foam mattress.

THE SAME STORY

By

Chukwuma Okoye-Nwaejiaga

If the overzealous class captain who loved literature so much had not ignored the protestations of the notoriously unserious members of the class and decided to go to the literature teacher's house to get him after they had waited in vain for him in the classroom, perhaps it would have been an entirely different story. Perhaps the story would have ended. But he had. So the story continued. The same story.

According to the class captain the class waited for its literature teacher for more than the regulation fifteen minutes after the hour. When he failed to show up he decided to go to his house and check him out. He felt perhaps that he might have forgotten. It was quite unlike him to be late or absent. Besides the teacher had mandated the captain to come and check him at home anytime he failed to come to class without prior notice, so he had to go.

He pressed on the doorbell awhile and getting no reply whatsoever, instinctively decided to look in through the window. Then he saw her folded on the couch, drenched in blood. He ran the entire one kilometre to the Principal's office. Desperately gasping for breath and struggling to contain his excitement he stammered his story to the Principal and the Bursar who was with him at the time. Obviously they were trying to find a way of keeping the students alive and in school after the government announcement of the withdrawal of all forms of feeding subsidy.

By the time the policeman arrived with an ambulance, the neighbours had already worked it out that he had eventually succeeded in killing her. After countless attempts, they mourned he finally succeeded in getting rid of her. One neighbour in particular swore she knew it was just a matter of time. She had told her husband about this impending murder but he had ordered her to keep quiet and mind her own business. If only he had believed her. Husbands rarely listened to their wives on such matters-or any matter at all. Poor woman thought the concerned neighbour. And she was so gentle and sweet; so pretty but oh so sad. Perhaps it was just as well... It was all over for her now. All the suffering; the sadness, the pain. Men... wickedness. She was glad her own husband was an exception to an appreciable extent.

The police arrived with an ambulance, heralded by a car with a wailing siren. The two vehicles screeched to a halt in front of the house, frantically dispersing all the excited groupings that had formed below the stairs, generating and exchanging opinions, hearsay, suggestions and gossip. By sheer creative ingenuity some of the group had actually arrived at the possible whereabouts of the dead woman's husband, the wicked man who murdered his wife in the dead of night and ran away. Anyway, it was a miracle the way the ambulance avoided running into the house. Some of the women who scurried out of its way just on time actually murmured curses at the driver, the witch who perhaps was not satisfied with only one death and longed for more. Some, however, advised him to look to his own mother for another death.

In an unprecedented display of efficiency, the policemen had the door broken down in no time at all. The woman was brought out on a stretcher. She was thoroughly covered in caked blood. Her mouth and neck had so much blood that it was as if she had not in fact been bleeding but drinking blood. She looked like a child who had sloppily splashed cereal all over herself in an attempt at feeding herself. To the delight of all, the very few who had the courage to get close enough announced that she was not dead. Yes! Indeed she was alive. She moved slightly and began to murmur incoherently all the way into the ambulance. The siren was switched on and as the crowd made way for the driver to put the vehicle into reverse one of the policemen shouted excitedly from the house. Soon her husband was brought out-dead. But what really shocked the policemen was the expression on his face. They couldn't stand it so they had to cover his face with the bed sheet as soon as he was laid on the stretcher. They had seen dead faces but none as alive as that. They drove off amidst much noise, dust and excitement. As the siren faded the people began to disperse reluctantly, each with his or her own special edition of the tragedy. The most enigmatic part was the body on the stretcher, which was totally covered. They could neither identify the body nor ascertain the cause of death.

When she came to hours later in the hospital, if indeed she did, she was silent. Upon examination the doctors surmised that she was in shock and had suffered a loss of memory. That meant that she could neither remember what happened nor tell anyone anything. The most curious of the doctor's diagnoses was that she had drunk a lot of blood-or must have, for there was so much blood in her system; and that she was one month pregnant. When her father arrived he quickly arranged for her transfer to a private and reputable hospital. In vain the doctors laboured to crack her wall of silence and indifference. She appeared to be in splendid health, even more beautiful than she had ever been. She wore an absolutely contented and peaceful expression; devoid of worry, sorrow or pain, all the ingredients that had characterised her life. She was a benevolent martyr; a forgiving saint... And the child within her grew well, almost eagerly. The child too seemed in surprisingly good health. So she was discharged after about two months. But her father brought home a nurse from the hospital to look after her. The endless doctors and psychiatrists had unanimously suggested that she might not only recover her memory but also her voice. The two, in fact, had become one. However they arrived at such duality. To her father 'may' was grossly inadequate. It was not good enough and offered no concrete hope to which one could hold onto. So, he resolved to search for some other cures.

He took his daughter to a native doctor, a renowned medicine man whose supernatural feats cut quite an impeccable record. After a thorough examination of the case, the doctor with the enormous insight submitted that she had seen more than the eye could see, and therefore had been silenced. He stated that when the eye had seen more than it was supposed to see then it shall not find the mouth with which to tell. In his own words she had had an 'eyeful'. According to him there are supernatural forces that play around, usually anonymously, in the affairs of man. She had been used by one of such forces. However, unlike some others who had been similarly used, she got so close that she could break the anonymity of this particular force. That was why she had been silenced. Her father, needless to say, neither understood nor trusted such an absolutely fraudulent diagnosis. And when the doctor asked for such ridiculous sacrificial materials as yards of white and red cloth, a piece of white chalk, a cock, a tortoise shell, a snail shell, two eggs and an aged woman's urine he failed to help the situation. It was a sheer waste of time. He had never really thought much of these traditional quacks. But he had to consult one just in case... He did not want to take any chances. Finally he brought her heart-rending silence home and was grateful to God at least for her good health and the apparent health of his unborn grandchild. He began to look seriously to the unborn, as if it held the key to the puzzle of the silence. And in fact it did, as he would come to discover later. Not that it exactly held the key to the puzzle, but in a way it held the key to the silence itself.

At the expected time her father took her to the maternity ward where she put to bed a rather cheerful and healthy baby boy. But the baby was strange in a way that none of the midwives could fathom. Anyway, after the baby was delivered and taken away by the midwives, she went into an exhausted deep sleep. When she woke up she noticed a bundle swaying in the cot beside her. The nurse in attendance smiled at her consciousness and lifted the bundle delicately from the cot.

"Congratulations," she said as she proffered the bundle to her. "It is a bouncing baby boy."

For the first time in a long while there appeared a flicker of a smile on her face. She opened her arms and received the bundle. Then she parted the cloth to look at the face of the baby boy. And there she held it in her arms: the horror of her life, come back to torment her and imprison her again in misery and madness. She began to scream hysterically, and before the nurse could stop her, she smashed the bundle violently against the concrete wall.

"He made me do it!" she screamed as she struggled to get off the bed. But she was too weak to get up. She fell back on the bed.

"He made me do it," she muttered weakly as she pointed at the lifeless bundle lying on the floor, gradually turning crimson with blood.

"He made me, ..." she muttered again faintly. Then she passed out.

BLISTERPACK OF MEMORIES

By

Sola Adeyemi

Gradually, I become aware of myself.

I am lying down in a moving vehicle that seems to be in a kind of procession. The procession is moving so slowly there must be a thousand vehicles involved. Trust the mid-day traffic in Lagos to be this difficult. But not quite like it. This traffic does not move in jerks and bumps, rather it is a steady slow roll as if the vehicles are in a kind of parade, or a funeral. Or maybe there is a funeral procession ahead. The infernal attitude of Lagosians. They no longer bury their dead only on weekends; they must disturb others in the course of mourning. Why, the other day, traffic was held up at Ikeja for more than two hours - and on a Monday morning for that matter - because the casket fell off the hearse, throwing the body into a murky gutter. People around said the dead man must have been very wicked when he was alive or else his corpse would not have come to such a disgrace.

But how did I get to be inside a moving vehicle? I should be on my bed at home, sleeping, or... I remember I went out yesterday. Was it yesterday? I can't remember very well. My brain is so fuzzy; I must have drunk quite a lot. I can recollect though that I went to a house in the outskirts of the city, towards the Badagry Township. I even drove myself because I remember asking for the way from a small boy selling sweets and *kola* nuts. Yes. I entered this white bungalow; a woman welcomed me and invited me inside. I can't remember any more. I can't even remember who the woman was, or her name. It must have been a dream.

Yet, I feel funny. Usually, if I have had a lot to drink, I wake up with a terrible hangover and a mammoth headache. But now, nothing. Not a single feeling. Only that this bed is different from my own. It is a little bit hard and somewhat on the small side – I can't even turn on my side. I dread opening my eyes. I can guess correctly what will happen. My head will reel and I will feel like throwing up.

Suddenly, I remember that I am supposed to keep an appointment with the Minister for 10 o'clock this morning. There is this deal I've being chasing for the past three months. It involves sand filling a portion of the swampy area by the lagoon and selling the land afterwards as either undeveloped or developed plots. I am to decide which would benefit us more -"us" meaning the Minister and myself. We've been on it for a long time now, with the Minister bickering over the 15% of the contract fee I offered him. He wanted a whopping 40%. Finally, he has come to his senses, with this current rumour of an imminent reshuffling of the Federal cabinet. He realises that he may not get anything after all if he does not act quickly.

The man intrigues me though. Always sacking his staff for one form of corruption or the other, even if it is still in the planning stage. He even called a press conference over a clerk who demanded - not collected, mind you -demanded a paltry sum of 100 Naira from a woman for 'services rendered'. Anyway, I have already decided: I shall offer him 25%.

But he doesn't like been kept waiting, so I have to get up. I cautiously open my eyes - Nothing. No feeling at all, no change at all! Everywhere is still as black as total blackout. I try to look outside but I find that I can't do that either. I try again, but it is not possible. I can't even move my head. Where am I? What is happening? I am in a supine position. I try to lift up my hands to my face but they are wrapped in a fluffy material that I can't see. My eyes are covered and my nose blocked by what feels like a wad of cotton wool. WHAT IS HAPPENING? I must get out of this nightmare, if it is one.

Hardly had that thought come to my mind when I find myself floating in the air. This must be one hell of a nightmare, I think.

But now, I can see. Suddenly, I look around me and see a long line of vehicles all draped in posters, moving along the road. What comes to me immediately is a political procession. Since the government lifted the ban on politics, the politicians have not let us rest, bombarding us daily with all sorts of gimmicks and ideas about how not to campaign. But, I can't complain. They are my friends. They will issue contracts when the elections are over, and I feed on contracts. But this procession is unreal: no rabble-rousing cries, no songs, no violence, no mayhem - so unlike my city. I look closely at a poster and see that it is an obituary notice. It even has the photograph of the deceased. One thing immediately strikes me about the picture – it looks so uncannily like me.

Just as I begin to ponder on this, the leading vehicle stops, forcing the others behind to follow suit. Some uniformed men come out of the vehicle, open the hatch-door and proceed to bring out a long white casket.

This grows more disturbing.

The men carry the casket up some wide steps and into a building, quite like the cathedral I attend. People come out of the other vehicles and follow the casket into the church.

Well, I sometimes am curious, particularly when I don't have anything more important to do. Now, my curiosity has been aroused. I have to get to the root of this mystery. The Minister can wait.

I follow the people inside the church.

A service is going on in the church. The choir is singing and some people in the church rise to their feet as the casket is brought in. But I can't hear anything they are singing. I can feel that they are singing and I can see them swaying from side to side, waving the pamphlets which they hold in their left hands like banners, but I can't hear any sound. Maybe it is a dumb show. Sometimes you get to be in these dreams where the whole experience is like a night of soundless, black and white film.

This does not bother me since I have already decided that I am in a dream. And dreams wouldn't be dreams if we could understand them. Anyway, if strange things don't happen in dreams, where else will they happen?

The casket is carried right up to the front area of the church, before the altar, and placed on a pedestal prepared for it. A man in black gown - a priest - holding a black bible moves up to the box, performs some mumbo-jumbo over it and signals the casket-bearers to open it. I move closer to them. Nobody asks me to move back. They apparently have not seen me, or they are ignoring me. Whichever, it suits me fine.

The men undo the latches holding the box and raise the lid. It opens onto a side held with hinges. I move closer still. The figure in the casket is all wrapped in a white cloth. The priest lifts the shroud on one end to reveal the face of the deceased. I feel a great pity rising up and overwhelming me because the man looks so young – he couldn't have been more than thirty years of age, thirty-five at the extreme.

Something is oddly familiar about the man though. He looks so much like me, in every way. Even to the scar on the chin. I study him more closely and realise with a frightful thump that the dead man is ME!

Or my twin brother. A clone!

There is this belief that men are created in pairs although they do not meet their 'mates' until they die, or in dreams. I wonder what killed my mate in this 'dream'.

The priest makes the sign of the cross over my mate. Then he moves up a short step-case into the pulpit and begins to utter such terrible things even I feel the shock.

"Such a reckless fool. It is better he died when he did. They all pretend to be so righteous and put on holier-than-thou attitudes. These young upstarts. Now, here is the President of their club, lying in a coffin, dead like a squashed mosquito, from *magun*. On another man's wife and so young too. So sad, I wish I were not officiating today. In fact, I am hungry and I am sure Sister Agnes is waiting for me. Ah, Sister Agnes...."

I look at the congregation to see how they are reacting to this strange sermon. But they all bend down. I turn my gaze back at the priest and realise with alarm that it is his thoughts I can hear! I feel disconcerted.

One woman in the front pew is saying something. I move towards her direction, at least to be away from the priest and his immoral thoughts. She resembles my wife.

"Stupid man. I feel like killing him all over again. Leaving me and the kids in the house on the pretence that he was going on a business trip only to go and die on top of that slut. It would have been better if he had died in an accident, but magun, and on an *Ashewo*. I won't ever live it down."

Suddenly, all around me, I hear a cacophony of voices, castigating, rebuking and, yes, even desiring the dead man. I try to shut my ears but it is not possible. I cannot even leave the church. So, I move closer to the coffin and continue to stare at the corpse. Still, the voices ring around me:

"...how I wish he had succumbed to my seductions..."

"...What a pity. And he was supposed to give me the capital to start my business yesterday..."

"...I wonder if I could attract his widow. She still looks very desirable..."

"...wrong with these young men. Ah, at his age, I was still struggling to pass my G.C.E. London Matriculations. He had everything..."

"...*Olosi, oloriburuku*, skirt-chaser, woman-wrapper. May you die many times over..."

"...If only I had agreed to go out with him. I hear he was generous to a fault..."

"...."

"...."

I cannot wait for this bizarre service to come to an end. It is becoming quite unnerving. I wonder if I didn't make a mistake by coming in here at all.

After a short while which actually seems like an hour, the congregation all stand up. The priest moves to the coffin and places an open bible on the chest of the corpse. At a signal, the casket-bearers close the coffin and bear it aloft, following the priest and the choir down the aisle. The congregation follow, led by that young woman who sat in the front row. Two small kids are on either side of her. I wait until the last man is out before leaving the church. I have had enough of the queer experience and my only wish now is to go home and wake up from this strange dream.

But, stranger things are yet to happen, for I suddenly find myself beside the coffin. The procession is going to the cemetery behind the church building.

The voices now become more boisterous, a gathering market in the afternoon of a wasted life. Everybody is speaking at the same time.

"...I wish this procession would move faster. I have a business appointment...." A young man.

"...I hope Sister Agnes is still waiting..." The priest. I hope so too, and may she give you an incurable VD.

"...Tunji said he would meet me here. I know he has gone to keep a date with Bisi..." A very unattractive and badly dressed woman. I sincerely hope so. One look at you and I would invent an appointment myself even if I didn't have one before.

"...Thank God for this man's death-O. I won't have to pay any dime to any hired assassin any more..." A man who closely resembles my best friend. May you rot, I feel like socking him a good one.

"...I must now get that contract. My main competitor is gone. All I need now is..." A bald-headed man. Sucker.

"...Ah, Banji. You promised to love me forever. So, here is the end of forever. And you haven't even bought the *Beast* for me..." A pretty young lady. Beast *ko*, Monster *ni*. And why did she have to mention **MY** name?

We arrive finally at a freshly dug grave. And after a short ceremony, the coffin is gradually lowered into the grave. I feel a sense of regret and loss. Such a young man. Apparently at the peak of his career, and he seems to have affected so many lives, but not a single tear is being shed for him. I wish he would resurrect and see the deceit of his so-called friends, and family.

I feel... I reel from an unexpected bombardment. Before I can regain my balance, another shattering set of blows hit me.

Then I understand what is happening. The young woman with the kids is being vindictive. She is shovelling soil onto the coffin and it is that effect that is so shocking.

Probably somebody knocking on my door. I'll soon wake up. Another series of thuds follow and I am buffeted right and left until...

I remember my childhood. There was a wardrobe at the foot of my big poster bed. I would dream that the wardrobe was full of sand and that the sand was being tipped over my helpless, prone body. I feel exactly the same way now.

Unable to help myself or resist the blows, I tumble into the yawning grave and feel my body being covered up. At the same time, a weird noise mixed with the chiming of a clangourous bell starts from somewhere in the recesses of my brain, rises in volume and intensity and continues to rise until it reaches an alarming crescendo...

I cry for help but nobody hears or heeds my call. A thousand stars hit my head and assail my vision. I twirl and tumble down, down, down....

I wake into unconsciousness....

FLIGHT 109

By

GANJA EKEH

"Good evening, this is your captain speaking.
Welcome aboard Nigerian Air Flight 109. The No-
smoking sign is now finally off, so feel free to light
cigarettes in the designated smoking areas and we
apologise for any inconvenience the delay has caused.
The delay was due to bad weather, but everything
should be fine now. We will be cruising at an altitude of
37 000 feet and should be making our first stop in Cairo
in five hours. After a re-fuelling stop there, our
destination, Syria, will be only three hours away."

"What?" "What?"

The passengers began to mumble and grumble
some began shouting. Flight 109 was scheduled to go
to Rome so what was this pilot talking about Syria?
"Abeg stop dis plane make I comot here!" the lady next
to me, demanded, "I go walk back go airport." It would
have been rather odd to drop her off there since we had
been flying for almost thirty minutes already, and over
water, no less. I was rather perturbed myself. I rang
the bell for a stewardess so I could find out what the hell
was going on. The stewardess arrived. She looked like
a plump crayon. It was the effect of over-bleaching her
skin. Her skin was really orange, but her slight beard,
dark in colour (with an underlying bluish hue),
contrasted sharply. "Can I 'elp yoew?" she asked in a
fake British cockney accent. Wanting to show that I,too,
had visited London, I retorted: "Yes, plyse, oi waws

jawst wowndering woahw 'appened. Oi waws uwnder the impresh'n that this floight woulwd be gawing to Rawme."

She was not to be outdone. "Well, the floight's bahyn rerouw'ehd toow Saiy-rya caws weey coow-oont get permish'n toow lahynd in Rawme. Weey're rayly sawry fowr the ayncownvynience sir" and with that she left, feeling triumphant in her stupidity.

I was aghast and would have been beside myself if the lady at my side wasn't already there. She seemed a feisty one, this lady. I watched her as she shuffled her feet uneasily and tied/untied her wrapper. Somebody should warn her that Europe was not Kongi, and it was cold there. For some reason she refused to use the overhead compartments to store her hand luggage. This made it really annoying and inconvenient for there was a certain smell coming from her large, white bag.

"Shet men! Gard dem it! I don noh worris strong wit dees peeps men. Shet! I mean. If dey was gonna gorra go to Siria, den dey shour have telled us men, shet! Dis is just silly men. Shet!"

I looked behind me at the man shouting. He had sleek Jeri curls and was wearing loads of gold. He looked the type who lived in America and came back home to Nigeria every two months on some dubious mission. I got the impression he thought he sounded equally American. He continued. "Tek me to de pilot, men, shet! I gorra talk to him men. He gorra know whas hup, dawg." The lady beside me wasn't having that. "Plis, sit down, Mista Maikeh Jahsin. Dis is not hamerica o! Look if you distob di plane driver and we crash, is me and you today." That set it off with the man. Oh yes.

Michael Jackson of Ayakoroma wouldn't allow any third-worlder to have the last word.
He blew up: "Hey shurrup men. I wasn't talking to you, men, silly bitch."

She might not have left Kongi before, but she knew what "bitch" meant to her. "Ehn? Bish? Me? Bish? Who are you calling bish? I wi' show you today." With that she stood up and removed her wrapper, tying it over her head, simultaneously revealing what I will politely describe as rainbow-coloured zebs. While these zebs ("underwear" to those who don't know) were the kinds that were given away freely with packets of Omo detergent, these particular zebs were unlike any underwear I had seen before. They seemed to magnify the lady's hips for some reason, and I could swear that it was impossible, proportion-wise, for her to be as big as that-if you understand what I'm saying to you. I tried to mediate.
 "Madam, please, don't mind him. He's just angry, please madam."

The other passengers were discontented with me. "I beg leave dem! Leave dem alone make dem fight!" The lady, buoyed by the fan-support, pushed me to my chair and took to the aisle ready to battle double space. Michael Jackson's ego would not allow him to back off and so he too took to the aisle. The audience roared its approval.
"Gi am!" "Punch am!" "Nack am one!" "*Oya*! Gi am *jare*!" they shouted. Your-captain-speaking came to the rescue with an announcement that would change all our lives in a few split seconds.

<cackle><cackle>"Er...this is your captain speaking. I would like you all to please listen carefully to what I have to say." The lady stopped in mid stride

whereupon Michael of Ayakoroma sat down promptly, seeing an avenue for escape. Your-captain-speaking continued: "I would like all of you to stay calm. This plane has been hijacked." The people stayed calm. The people started screaming. I had never heard so many different things at once:

"Oh Jesus of Nazareth! Ye who created the world in seven days. Alpha and Omega!"

"Ahhh...*won ti pa wa*! We have all die! They have kill us! Ahhh! Ahhh! We have die!"

"Kai! Wala-hi talai!"

And to finish the chorus was our 'English-speaking' air hostess whom I heard hiss under her breath "Nna, ehn? Abeg, whish wan be dis na."

After a considerable length of time the captain spoke again. "I would request that each passenger sit down and not move. The hijackers are four in number and are armed. Three of them will now come from the cockpit to give instructions. Please do as they say and we will all live."

•   •   •   •

As the hijackers ordered, we were all huddled in the back of the plane, but still the lady wouldn't let go her white bag. I wondered what would possess four men to hijack a plane, using slingshots, or "katapots" as the lady with the bag had said.

"Plis, Mr. I-Jack," she had said, "doesn't shoot me with your katapot O!"

This had to be the most unrefined hijacking operation that ever was. The problem was that even if we overpowered the three sling-shot-wielding hijackers, the last one could harm the pilot in the cockpit and our lives would be in jeopardy. They all wore masks and despite their crude weapons, did look rather dangerous. One of them began to speak.

"You people should count yourselves lucky, nay, blessed to be a part of this historic occasion." He was articulate and sounded, as they would say, well studied. "We are a group known as Movement for Military Rule and are dedicated to returning the country from it's corrupt civilian rulers who have siphoned all our money, back to military rule under strict discipline."

I was confused, or more appropriately, they were.

"Excuse me," I interjected, "but don't you have this backwards? The country *is* under military rule right now."

The hijackers looked at each other. "You're lying!" one of them barked at me.

"No, is true sah!"

Someone helped me out. The hijackers seemed stunned. They huddled together and had a mini-conference amidst heated whispers and vigorous head-movements. They turned around.

"What flight is this?" one asked.

"Nigerian Air flight 109 orig..."

"Nigerian Air? Nigerian Air?" All three of them immediately hissed. The first one removed his mask and sighed. The other two followed suit as all of us watched in amazement. They stood there shaking their heads. "Nigerian Air? How did we end up on Nigerian air?" They sat down dejectedly. "Sorry" the lady with the bag consoled them.

"Sorry ehn," others joined in.

Everyone seemed genuinely distraught at the turn of events. This is a trait of Nigerians—if someone else has the catapult, you sympathise with them when they need the sympathy. It's just the way things work.

A plan was forming in my head, but I was interrupted as the first of the three said, "Well, I guess I'll go get the one with the pilot and we'll all leave you people alone".

"No wait!" I shouted, "You can still accomplish something." Everyone looked at me as though I was crazy, but I smiled knowingly. This was a once in a lifetime opportunity.

●   ●   ●   ●

"<Yawn> When do you think they'll reply?" the first hijacker asked. "Oh, I don't know. Probably an hour or so..." I said, looking around. The two other hijackers, Michael Jackson, the feisty lady, and a high-school kid were playing Scrabble in the lounge. This is what it looked like, a game of Scrabble. Deep down I knew that living humans on this earth had, ever heard very few words on that board. But they seemed to be into the game. Other passengers were generally lounging and relaxing, several getting to know each other and telling jokes. I wondered if the pilot was on to what was going on. I hoped not. The hijacker in the cockpit had not revealed anything to him. I looked at my watch; we'd been flying for three hours. We'd need to refuel in two.

"Quiet! Quiet! It's the news!" someone shouted. We all rushed, our hearts beating, to the different radios in the cabin, and listened:

"This is an international news flash. A group calling themselves the Movement for Democracy has hijacked a Nigerian airliner bound for Syria. In a radioed relay to the Nigerian authorities, the hijackers have demanded the immediate release of several Nigerian political prisoners and the immediate instalment of yet another president-elect who is now in prison after an annulled election."

Everyone in the cabin cheered. I smiled. The news continued. "Reports say that among the passengers is the son of the country's Military president who is being held chief hostage." Everyone cheered. I bowed to my audience. "Presido! Presido!" some chanted, but I was not having that. I didn't want to follow in my father's footsteps. The news ended on a positive note, for us at least.

"The Nigerian government is taking the hijackers demands very seriously as they are reported to be heavily armed and extremely dangerous." I looked at the catapult. Well, it was on his arm and somewhat dangerous - to squirrels. As soon as the news ended there was endless banter, but an air of optimism prevailed. We shook hands. We were doing, in a plane, something that several million people had tried to do on the ground, but failed.

"Arise o Compatriots..." someone started singing. We sang the rest of the anthem all standing solemnly and hoping for the best - different tribes though we were, we stood in one accord: One people bound in Freedom, Peace and Unity.

•   •   •   •

CAIRO AIRPORT: Security Lounge.

I watched as they led the lady with the white
bag away. She had been carrying a dead baby loaded
with drugs in the bag as well as several parcels of
heroin in her custom-made underwear. That was
disgusting. The hallway was empty and I felt cold. But
no one would give me a blanket. If the plane had landed
in Nigeria, as opposed to Cairo, perhaps things
would have been different. I have connections at home.
Here I am subject to a different law.
"Step this way please sir."
I stepped forward. The handcuffs hurt my wrists, but
that was not the real pain. The real pain was being
betrayed by the people I had tried to help. They had all
wanted to save themselves, and so decided to implicate
me. They said I masterminded the operation. But
hadn't they helped me out? Didn't they all try to seize
the opportunity too? I shook my head. The people I
loved had betrayed me. As I was escorted into the
INTERPOL vehicle, the cameras attacked me with their
flashes. The son of the President of Nigeria, a criminal.
An opportunist who turned a hijacking-gone-wrong
to a hijacking-of-purpose. The son of the President of
Nigeria. The son of a thief. For some I was just another
news item. For millions, I was a hero. Nigeria
We Hail Thee, Our Own Dear Motherland...

THE SIGN OF THE CRAB

By

Kolapo Oyefeso

July 15th 1988

Today is my twenty-first birthday. I am an adult now and I wish everybody would realise this. Auntie Sade gave me this five-year diary. It's a nice diary, blue and gold, but not what I expected. Auntie Sade is very rich and I expected something more. I think she saw I was disappointed because she told me that she has been keeping diaries for fifteen years. She says it's like having a best friend you can tell all your secrets to. I like the idea. At least the diary won't laugh at me, or tell my secrets to anyone else.

People are always saying I am stupid when I tell them things, and that I don't know what I am talking about. I think it is they who don't know what they are talking about.

I have to think of a place to hide my diary, to keep it from prying eyes.

I had a small party. Mummy insisted. I wore my new dress with the gold buttons. It has small brown and white squares, and a slit skirt. Everybody said it looked very nice. My cousins came and some friends from school. Mummy made *moin-moin* and *jollof* rice with *dodo* and fried chicken. Uncle Segun brought some beer and some of the boys got a bit rowdy and made a lot of noise. The nasty woman in the downstairs flat complained and cursed loud enough so we could hear. I hate this place. I hate Yemetu. I wish we could move to another part of Ibadan.

Mike did not come. I didn't tell him because it's like he is more my boyfriend than I am his girlfriend. He did not remember my birthday. And we talked about birthdays a few weeks ago. He wants one thing from me and he is not going to get it. He never takes me out and I haven't met any of his friends. If he thinks I am not good enough, that is his problem.

I like Auntie Sade. She is my best friend. She says I can stay with her anytime I want, at her house in Bodija. She is alone most of the time now, since armed robbers killed Uncle Tom and Titi went to England. She has many friends though, and they wear nice clothes and go to lots of parties. She buys dresses for me and gives me money. And, secret! secret! She has promised me a ticket to England when I graduate. Mummy doesn't know yet and she won't know till it's too late for her to say things like, 'Sade, don't you think...'

Things I need – a new boyfriend
                – new clothes and shoes
                – books for my literature project
                – someone to tell Mummy that I am old enough to live on campus.

September 28th 1988

I have been busy and I keep forgetting to write. I want to be a writer and writers should keep diaries; I read that somewhere. I will write, I promise.

Daddy came to see me today. He likes it that I am in the hostel. He prefers it to visiting the house. I hope I'll see more of him now. That will be good after the begging and arguing and the promises I made to

Mummy before she allowed me to move to the hostel. Mummy can be so difficult. But a deal is a deal. As long as my grades are good I'll stay on campus. That shouldn't be too difficult.

I like my father. He is tall and handsome and can make people laugh but... He came with his new wife in a new second-hand car. He must be making money now. He never had any before. Can't forget those bad times. Mummy wasn't working, and Daddy didn't give her money. Shouting and fighting every day. Tunde and I hiding in a corner as still as statues, afraid, too scared to do anything, watching and listening to them. I hated it, hated it so much. Tunde was always crying. I was happy when Mummy told Daddy to move out. Enough, she said first, then: lawyer, divorce.

And going back and forth to the High court. I think the divorce was a relief to Daddy. He was happy in court. The things they said! Lazy, irresponsible, other men, other women, marital rights, sex! So embarrassing. I used to hide my face. Sometimes I wanted to talk, to shout even, but in court you speak only when they call you. And nobody called me. Besides, the lawyers had so much to say there was no time for anyone else. It seems like such a long time ago, not like three years at all. If I didn't want to write so much, I think I would have liked to be a lawyer; then people will always listen to me.

And Daddy forgot about us after the divorce. He moved to Lagos to live with the woman who had a son for him. Now he is married to another woman – a girl really, only a bit older than me. When I saw her today (the first time) I wanted to kick her. I hate her. Her skin is bleached and has dark patches and she looks like a prostitute.

Daddy may not be the best husband in the world but he knows how to make me feel better when I am sad. He can be very funny and we laugh and everything is all right. I like him a lot but he doesn't know anything about women.

School was boring today and I am feeling sad.
I need someone to love me. I need a friend.

January 17th 1989

Mama died yesterday. At eighty-five. I cried and cried. I am going to miss her, and Tunde will too. So good to be with and we loved her. Living with her was nice. She was funny and wise. That sounds like a rhyme, maybe I should write poetry too, especially now that I am half-sad and half I don't know what (don't really like poetry though. It's doesn't feel like serious writing).

Mama. All your jokes and lessons and stories of Ibadan and trading with your mother and travelling and missionaries and schools and holding us by the hand: walk briskly, don't drag your feet, look where you are going, are you feeling better, drink your *ogi*, eat your *eko*, have more *akara*. And that old, old man you took us to, who spoke like an *oyinbo* and taught us English and made us read and write over and over. The man who said that knowledge was power and the problem with Nigeria was that too many people were comfortable with ignorance. It is because of you and him that I want to be a writer.

When you fell ill and lost so much weight – I used to think you were so big and then suddenly I was bigger than you – and Mummy took you to *UCH* but the workers went on strike and then she took you to all those private clinics and spent so much money (they prescribed so many drugs, we could have opened a pharmacy with the drugs Mummy bought) then you told her to stop buying medicines and paying doctors because you were going home to meet your Lord; I knew you were going to die but I hoped and prayed.

School has been closed 'till further notice' and I am back at home. The non-academic staff is on strike and we were told to go home. It's strike, strike, strike everywhere these days and school is a long holiday with short breaks for work.

Mummy is very upset. Now that her mother has died, she must be feeling like an orphan. I didn't know how to console her, and so many people kept coming, so I went out and spent the day with my friends.

Things I do not need
– a lot of people sitting around pretending to be sad.
– relatives who think they can order me around.

March 6th 1989

I went to a new nightclub yesterday with Lara and her boyfriend. I don't have a boyfriend now (poor me!) so I tag along. Mike and I broke up when he said there must be something wrong with me because I wouldn't have sex with him.

Good idea: All boys should be lined up and shot – except my brother, and maybe, Yinka.

Secret: Yinka is a fine – very fine – boy in my department, and he has been looking at me a lot.

The club is called Larry's bar. I wonder who Larry is. Someone should talk to him. It is somewhere in New Bodija. It was full of boys. It is always full of boys I hear – the kind who should be shot – drinking, smoking and making a lot of noise. There was only one other girl and Lara and I did not want to stay but her boyfriend insisted. The boys argued about politics, religion and sex. Boys talk about sex a lot. They laugh about it. Maybe they don't like it very much, or they like it too much and are embarrassed to say so. Or maybe it's women they don't like. They went on and on. One ego-trip after another. Someone used that word on me recently. Checked it up. It fits boys and men. Ego-trip: 'e goes tripping. They trip a lot. About town, in their heads, over their tongues. Sometimes I think shooting would be too good for them. They should be made to clear drains and rubbish dumps, and build roads for the rest of their lives maybe then they will learn something. Lara says it isn't their fault. She says they are not grown up yet. I don't think so. They have had enough time to learn a few things. Mummy once complained about an old man misbehaving, and Uncle Segun told her that because a man has grey hair does not mean he is wise or mature. It only means he has grey hair.

School started three weeks ago and we have had exams this last week. I did not read much. We were not taught much – no time – but I could have read more than I did. The way school keeps going off and on makes it difficult to study. Even lecturers find it disturbing. I hope I pass.

○

March 12th 1989

Mama was buried today. I stood at the edge of her grave watching the earth fall in. I did not cry. Mummy and Auntie Sade cried and I thought I should but I was not feeling sad anymore. I know that Mama is happy wherever she is.

June 2nd 1989

A boy told us a story today about an accident at Iyaganku, between a truck full of mobile policemen and the escort of a senior military officer, a *GOC*. The mobile policemen – Mopol, he called them – were coming from the press centre in their usual wild fashion; they sing loudly, hang onto the sides of the truck and wave machine guns about like poor children with new toys.

The GOC was on the major road. No siren because there was no traffic. As his convoy came round the bend just before the press centre junction, the police truck shot onto the road, swerving wildly. The motorcyclist leading the convoy was swept into a ditch, and the car following the motorcycle ran into the side of the truck.

The boy who told the story is one of these people who make a story funny by acting it out while telling it. He was all over our room, waving his arms and playing both sides of the accident. "When *godo-godo* don jam GOC, all of *dem com'* scatter for road, com' begin *hala*." We laughed and laughed. He said the GOC ordered that the mopol be arrested, which was good for them. Everybody hates them. If it had been a normal, average Nigerian; someone who 'suffer don *dabaru 'im* sense' as Fela says, the mobile police, after running into the car, would have destroyed it, beaten him or her and carried the unlucky person away to some cell.

Our exams start next week if nothing serious happens before then. I have been doing a lot of work and they shouldn't be a problem. Mummy came last week with provisions and money. Business is good and I'm glad for her. She is happier now. She said, 'all thanks be to God.' Which reminds me, I went to church last Sunday with Ada. A new church. One of these

Pentecostal or 'born-again' churches. The service was entertaining. At one point, I wasn't sure if I was in church or at the Arts Theatre. The pastor was loud and intense but I couldn't feel any real message. He said 'Praise the Lord' and 'Aayymen' many times. I enjoyed the show. People weeping and wailing boisterously. I don't think they gnashed their teeth – if they did they must have done it quietly. They spoke in tongues though, starting and stopping as the pastor dictated. Demons were cast out with a lot of noise, and money collected several times. To be born again you have to dance to the altar, give your life, and then the pastor saves you. The band plays soft music and you float back to your seat, newly born. The pastor and his second-in-command spoke in funny American accents, one high-pitched, the other drawling – 'y'all gonna seeee da work of Gawd. Gawd bless y'all'.

Someone told me later that everyday, more of these churches appear. Like a rash.

I must remind Auntie Sade that it is my birthday next month.

August 1st 1989

My birthday came and went. Auntie Sade gave me cloth for two dresses and I am going to try that new tailor in Mokola. He made a beautiful *Shaba* skirt for Lara. Mummy invited a few people to the house. It was very quiet and nothing much happened.

Everybody is talking politics nowadays. Politicians are making a lot of noise and spending money. Some of Auntie Sade's friends are also friends to politicians and she hears all sorts of stories and rumours.

A man and a woman tried to *'419'* Mummy. She said these well-dressed people walked into her shop and offered to supply Bournvita at a low price. They told her they bought it from a director of Cadbury, from his special allocation. The deal was she had to buy a truckload to get the special price. She said they spoke nicely and smiled a lot and she didn't feel there was anything wrong. She calculated the profit and then spoke to some other traders about it. They agreed to buy the Bournvita and it was delivered a few days later. While the kaya were offloading the truck and the traders were carrying off their supplies, one of them opened a tin to mix a drink for her child. She cut the aluminium foil and found that the tin was full of sand and wood shavings. She screamed and the tricksters who were busy stuffing money into a bag heard her. They dropped the bag and ran. *Agbeni* is a busy market and *ole! ole!* was all it took for a crowd to chase them. They were caught, beaten severely, stripped naked and paraded through the market to the police station.

Mummy said that some people wanted to burn them, and it would have been cheaper to do so because the traders had to pay the police to hand back the money. They were going to hold it as evidence.

Daddy came to see Tunde and I. He stayed outside the house and would not come in. His second-hand car now looks its age. Bits and pieces of it are ready to drop off. He looked old too and his clothes were not up to their usual standard. His shoes had scuffmarks and he has lost weight. He talked and laughed a lot and gave each of us twenty Naira. He promised to see us every month and drove off in a cloud of smoke. Mummy watched from a window. She said that he did not look very well. I hope there isn't anything wrong with him. I wish he would take better care of himself. I miss him a lot, yet sometimes I get so angry when I remember all he did – or didn't do – that I feel I hate him.

I need my father, and my family, laughing and happy around me.

September 8th 1989

I am now going out with Yinka. He took me out a few times and comes to see me almost every day. That can only mean we are going out. He hasn't tried or even said anything about sex so maybe I am assuming too much. But I don't think so. He's really nice and I like him.

October 6th 1989

School started today. My final year. I can't wait to be out. No more school and no one hassling me. Auntie Sade said again that she would pay for a holiday in England when I graduate. I can't wait.

Yinka's sister, who works in Lagos, bought a second-hand car. A *'Tokunbo'* Toyota. She now travels up and down the expressway at all times. Yinka said his mother warned her about travelling alone after dark and she replied that her car was covered by the blood of Jesus. His father, who was listening, looked up and said, "Oh, is that what it is? I thought it was rust!" I laughed till it hurt.

I think Yinka likes me a lot. I like him and, secret! I have been thinking of having sex with him. I have to start sometime. I am almost twenty-three. I feel odd – not just odd, foolishly behind – when other girls talk about sex, some of them younger than me. I feel left out. Am I afraid? I don't think so. I have been close to it. I have urges, then there is a voice.

Is that voice mine, or Mummy's?

Yinka is not insisting but I think I should get it over and done with. It's becoming an embarrassment — my virginity.

November 17th 1989

We have a new literature lecturer. He is the most uninspiring teacher I have ever had. He teaches us African Literature and his criticisms and interpretations are always confusing. We all ignore everything he says.

Titi came home from England a week ago. I spent the last weekend with her and Auntie Sade. I had an exciting but exhausting time. We talked for hours. She told me all about her school, boyfriends, parties, the shops in London. Titi smokes, and drinks alcohol. I tried both — my first time. Made me dizzy at first but after a while it didn't feel so bad. We had a good laugh over it and she said I must come and stay with her in London.

Titi's language is shocking. My ears were hot and if I were lighter, it would have shown on my face. She used words that I never have. She used them for emphasis, freely. Like fuck, fucking or fucked, and shit (plain, or as bullshit, horseshit or jackshit). The funny thing is that after a few hours I found myself using these words. After twenty-four hours with her, I was liberated; swearing as if my tongue was heat-resistant and choking on cigarettes and alcohol.

Thinking about it, I'm glad that she wasn't into worse things. I'm sure I would have tried anything, awed by her as I was. I found it impossible to say no to her. I was sick for two days. She is going back to England next week and I'll be glad to see her go. Her lessons in modern lifestyle are a bit too much for me.

Jan 8th 1990

The new decade started with a grating sound. We went to church on New Year's Eve and the car had an accident on the way back. It was a depressing thing to happen but we soon got over it.

I am not sure what really happened but one of Auntie Sade's friends said that *IBB* played a trick on the politicians and they are all upset. But all they can do is grumble. Quietly.

Is this a secret? Maybe. Anyway, I had sex – or fucked, as Titi would say. Two nights ago. I felt so low afterwards. I went back to my room and covered myself up on my bed. I felt used, bruised, robbed, and dirty. But I also felt, yeah! I have done it!

I wonder why people make so much of sex. I don't think I will do it again soon. I don't like anyone being that close to me, the intrusion into my privacy, into me.

Yinka is coming here today and I don't know how I am going to look him in the face. I feel less than I was three days ago. Maybe this is what everybody feels and they get over it. Maybe one day I'll be like Titi and it will not mean anything at all. Right now I feel that if I never see another man in my life, it will be too soon.

I need another hymen, preferably intact. Or a shoulder to cry on. Or, if all fails, a strong drink.

NAME YOUR PRICE

By

Sola Osofisan

The young lady who waited by the roadside appeared to be expecting something, a taxi perhaps. One decelerated. She ignored it. The sun's setting emanations lingered longingly on her sparingly covered body. The evening breeze fondled her mostly artificial crop of hair. A professionally painted fingernail scratched a tiny birthmark on the tip of a crafted nose.

Another taxi slowed down.

She ignored it.

Passers-by stared: the old folks wore knowing looks; the hot-blooded young men gawked even as their tired wives envied the generous depth of cleavage the lady haughtily displayed. The young lady turned a blind eye to all of them.

She'd waited only a few minutes, but several types of luxury car had gone out of their way to honk their invitation to her. Still she waited. She had chosen a strategic position. And there was adequate space around her for cars to park without obstructing the sparse traffic.

She waited.

A white BMW 7 series noisily screeched its way around the corner. The young lady glanced up and interest flashed in her eyes. A faint smile warmed her cool features.

The car roared past, its windshield and rear splashed with multi-coloured stickers from many countries. Hip-hop music gushed out of its open windows.

Two blocks down, the car braked sharply, leaving smoking wheel marks on the road. The young man behind the wheel adjusted his rear view mirror to see the girl better. Seemingly satisfied, he reversed the car rapidly, skidding to a halt in front of her. He turned down the music, shoved up dark glasses to uncover bleary eyes and leaned out of the window, towards the girl. "Name your Price', he said. His affected drawl and the gum he chomped like a third rate whore gave his voice a fuzzy quality.

The lady doubled to peer through the open window. "Sorry", she said, "What did you say?".

"Don't muck around with me", he rasped impatiently, like one accustomed to having his way. He suddenly looked his age, a petulant twenty-three? "I gat no time to burn. Name a price and let's go play ball".

"It seems we have a poet here", the lady replied, her expression changing from curiosity to the forewarning of indignation. "My price?" she asked, stepping backwards, "Is this a market place? Or do I look like I'm for sale?"

Everything in skirt has a price, baby", the young man countered through a fit of derisive laughter spurred by the girl's retreat. "Were you expecting me to offer you a ride, instead of the more direct approach? Come on, the world is changing! You're too young to be so stale. How much? Even my mother has a price!"

"Well, go and buy your mother!", the young lady snapped and turned away.

The man began to laugh. "You look like the result of cross-breeding, a bitch with intelligence. Okay, let's know what you're saying. What's your game?"

She hesitated. A smile, that of someone who had an ace tucked up the secret warmth of a bra cup. "Who owns this Car?"

The question flipped him. "What's it to you who owns the car? Are you playing ball or not?"

"I may", she encouraged, teasing him with the most seductive smile in a vast arsenal, and the outward thrust of riveting flesh. "If you tell me who owns this car, I just might play ball. In fact, I do feel like it"

He realized the irritation now visible on his face was thrilling her. "Well, for your information, Miss Curious, its mine. The product of my hard work." He didn't like the cocky assurance of the mischievous smile that now played on her lips. He didn't feel easy with the fire that seemed to burn in each of her eyes like mysterious stars.

"What would a little man like you know about hard work? Or you meant some other kind of hardness. Hard substances for instance"?

"You could get your pretty face rearranged for saying a stupid thing like that." He was livid now. He started the engine. "Others have died for saying much less"

"Don't tell me you're offended". She pouted playfully, a mother teasing a baby in an oversized crib. "We have such a sensitive skin, don't we? To catch a lion, you have to enter the jungle". She shook her wild mane, taunting the core of his pride with her smile. "I am a lion. And my price, just in case you're still keen, is this lovely ride of yours. You wouldn't be able to afford so much, would you?"

He switched off the engine. "My car?" He looked incredulous for a moment, then the self-assurance flooded back. "You want a car like this devil for a quick hump in the dump?" His mouth hung open.

"You have a right to be vulgar," she countered sweetly. "For your information, I don't want a car like this baby here. I want this particular devil. You can't begin to imagine what I have to offer. I could take you to heaven"

"Or hell!"

"Depends on where you want to go"

He stepped out almost without being aware he was doing so, and looked at her again across the roof of the car. He shook his head in disbelief. "What's so hot about you anyway?"

"That's for you to find out"

"Aren't you made of the same stuff I pick up every time I feel like leaving my current steady for a little bit of adventure?"

"I am all that and much more. You may have had many, but believe me, you're no expert until you've had all."

The rest of the world had become a distant blur to the young man. "I'm getting highly tempted", he said.

"Judas probably said that two thousand years ago."

He burst into laughter again. "Hey, I think you ought to be on tee-vee. You've got style."

"I know", she answered. "You stopped. I didn't call you. You asked for my price. Now that you know how expensive I am, what are you going to do about it?"

"Are you daring me?"

"Why not?"

"Hop in"

"Now you're talking". She giggled gaily as she slipped into the car beside him. "My price is the car, remember?"

"Forget the joke and let's be two serious people for a second. I know a cosy hotel that is out of-"

"No", she stopped him. "When I go on a trip, I pick a point. I know many places. Just drive. I'll direct you. Satisfaction guaranteed."

He threw the car into gear and shot away. "This is a totally different experience", he muttered.

"That's part of the service. You just have fun while it lasts. You're paying. Turn left here"

He obeyed.

"We're heading for Victoria Island?"

"Yes."

"A house?"

"No. A Pig Farm. What kind of question is that?"

The young man erupted into fresh laughter, punching the wheel excitedly. Tears welled up in his eyes. "You know", he gasped, "If you weren't in this messy biz, you would fit the image of my soul mate. Gracefully tall, slim, certainly head-turning and fast on the uptake. I like a girl who can hold her own. You're sharp".

"Thanks". She fished a crumpled cigarette pack out of her tiny bag, stuck a stick in her mouth and lit it with his gold lighter. She puffed contentedly for a silent moment.

"Do you always wait to be picked up at that same spot?" he ventured again.

"I've never used the same place twice. Parties, high-class clubs and hotels, different places depending on my mood. I was on the street as a sort of homage to this game. Today means a lot to me. And I don't get picked up. I've got style. I do the picking"

"Is today some kind of anniversary? Your birthday?"

She didn't answer. Thinking she didn't want personal questions, he changed the subject. "Why did you play so hard to get back there? I intend to pay for services rendered you know? Treat the customer right, they say"

She twisted around on the bucket seat to face him, curling up. Her miniscule skirt scooted up, revealing more flesh. She didn't smile. "I am hard to get", she said seriously. "So, what do you do?"

"Uh huh. You're a pro. You know the rules. No personal questions. They only get in the way of a hello-goodbye bang. Strings complicate simple things."

"I suppose you're right", she admitted. A faraway haze crept into her eyes as she ran them across the stickers that could now be read in reverse. Countries of the world. "I guess I like you in a no-strings sort of way. You're obviously a traveller. I like adventurous men.

"Oh, I travel a lot!" he said brightly, seeming to inflate behind the wheel. "I've been to every country that matters"

She reached out the window and tried to peel off one of the stickers. "Do you have to deface such a nice car with so many stickers? You don't have to advertise your travels, you know?"

"I believe in self-promotion", he said through amused laughter. "They'll come off easily anyway"

"Thank goodness", she heaved and withdrew her hand.

"Why did you say that?"

"Say what?"

"Why did you say 'Thank goodness'?"

A pause. She seemed to be weighing his question on some unseen scale. Instead of an answer, she said, "Turn left."

He did.

"Now, go right"

He obeyed.

Silence.

"Do you sniff? I have good stuff if you're keen".

The girl shrugged indifferently. "I do whatever I fancy. Nothing serious" She threw him a glance. "Nothing in your class".

He smiled vaguely.

"I was right then. I was right about the kind of hard work you do" It wasn't a question, so he didn't respond.

"I can smell your type a mile away," she said.

"Turn left"

Left.

"I am not too easy to please. If you give me a good time, I could keep you in comfort for a while."

"You're so generous," she sneered. More of the steel in her flashed briefly. "That won't be necessary, thank you". She knelt on the seat to rummage through the pile of magazines on the back seat.

"What are you looking for?"

"The ladies'"

He went into another fit of laughter. "Oh God, I haven't laughed this much in ages." He brushed off the tears in the corners of his eyes.

The girl was smiling. "I like a man who has a good sense of humour. It means apart from laughing at the foolishness of the world, he can also laugh at himself. That's the kind of man I hope to find when I settle down"

The young man yanked his foot off the accelerator as if it had suddenly grown hot. "You mean..." The shock was scrawled all over his face. "You mean people like you marry and make babies like normal people?"

"Why not?"

"Horror!" he exclaimed, smacking himself on the head. "Who'd marry you?"

"It doesn't gauge mileage you know? I've done my time. I'm just about through gathering money to comfortably establish myself anywhere I choose. I plan to hook a man and start a family"

"Hook is the word sister". He fired the engine again, shaking his head in wonder and perhaps pity for the man who would marry the girl. "Where do I go here?"

"Right. Drive to the end of the close"

As they turned, the car's wheels crunched the dry leaves and twigs that had fallen from the overhanging canopy of trees. There were six houses in the cul-de-sac, three on either side. All warned the world to beware of dogs, except the last house on the right. It appeared new, unlived in.

The young man stopped the car. "I'm not familiar with this area", he said.

"I am", said the girl. "Come on". She stepped out of the car.

A security man in front of one of the houses watched them with bored eyes, his back pressed to a tree. He was motionless, quiet... like the close. Only the breeze fanning the trees made a whooshing noise that sounded like the frenzied whispering of anxious spirits.

The young man sprung open a concealed compartment under the dashboard and removed a small tin. He quenched the tape player and followed the girl through the gate of the new house, shaking his bunch of keys expectantly. He felt like a teenager about to discover hands-on the ancient secrets of womanhood. He followed the girl to the boy's quarters at the back of the house.

"Do you use this place often?"

"I never use a location more than once. At least, not since the last two months when I decided to secure retirement. Body no be wood, you know? I'm no longer sixteen."

She felt above a window for a key.

"How old are you?"

"Old enough". She unlocked one of the three doors. "Old enough to know I'm old enough to do something else with my life"

As the young man moved to enter, he stopped abruptly. He thought he'd seen a shadow recoiling from one of the dust-layered windows. "Whose house is this?"

"Shhh", she hushed with a reassuring smile. "No questions, remember?"

"What if the owner appears?"

"He won't. He's out of town"

"Don't they have a security man or something watching the place?"

She was growing irritated. "You ask too many questions. Am I a baby, or would I bring you to a place where you're likely to be embarrassed? It's not too late to back out, you know"

He entered the room.

She followed, switching on a lonely bulb that pushed back the dusk fast encroaching outdoors. A large bare mattress filled the whole floor in one corner. There was nothing else. The young man couldn't hide his disappointment.

"Is this all?"

"What else do you expect? This is hello-goodbye, remember? A bed is all you need".

"We could have gone to a five star hotel-"

"A bed is a bed anywhere"

"This is not a bed. It's just a mattress that's looking for someone to lie on it"

"We will"

"Don't you want wine, good music, food, a little romance...?"

She paused, a quizzical look on her face. "You want to woo me, get me to like you, and then you go away? Is that what you want?"

"No. Nothing like that".

"Believe me, I'll be okay for you here. Memories, you know? It's a reminder of where the first man I ever picked up took me. It was a backdoor place like this". She went for him with sensitised fingertips, massaging the tension out of his neck and shoulders. "Besides, isn't performance all you're interested in?"

He shrugged out of his T-shirt.

He helped her undress.

His car keys fell to the floor beside the mattress as their legs yielded and they crashed on the foam.

He took a little heroin from the small tin.

She declined.

He brought out a Gold Circle from a pack in his pocket, just in case...

She teased him.

He used it anyway.

They bit and tore at each other's flesh forever, and at the end of time, it really was the best sex he'd ever had. Words failed to express the strange paths she had guided him through with experienced confidence. She'd taken him to heaven.

Later, naked on the mattress, sucking on a cigarette he had lifted from her crumpled pack, he wondered, "what's a smart babe like you doing in a messy business like this?"

She smiled secretly as her mind unlocked the gates of memory. "It started as a kick, a game with the other girls back at school. It became a necessity when my personal economy suffered a depression. But as I grew older, I realized I couldn't go on forever. Men like you who keep us in business lose interest when age begins to tell. So, in the last few weeks, working with a few men I'd run into over the years, the game became an effective means of gathering good money

She paused to look directly into his eyes. "Now, fools like you donate generously"

The young man momentarily wondered why she'd called him a fool. Was it another game? The door flew open at that moment and three hefty men barged into the room. One held a black pistol. He was the security man they had seen outside. The other two slashed the air with ugly-looking daggers.

The young man was grabbed as he scurried for his discarded clothes. A knife tip drew a little blood from his nipple to remind him of the worth of silence. He became numb, eyes bulging, barely able to stand on his own feet.

The girl slipped back into her tiny skirt; unflustered by the hungry looks the three men gave her clashing breasts.

"What do you want from me", spluttered the young man.

She picked up his car keys.

"Our deal still stands, remember? You have the fun, I have the car. There's a buyer waiting. Your car will cross the border before this night is done. And so will you, although you'll be crossing elsewhere".

The young man's face was a terrified mask. His body shook and his mouth worked, desperately trying to shape elusive words. "Take... take the car... Dddddon't hurt me..."

A burly hand stuffed the young man's pants into his mouth.

"I'm a smart girl, friend. You admitted that much yourself. You've been to heaven. Now, it's time for hell".

She nodded to the men.

They closed in on the man who exploded into tears.

The girl waved with the keys and left.
A knife rose.

THE DEAL

By

Wale Okediran

The mortuary was as usual: cold, damp and smelled of the eye-stinging fumes of Formalin. As Linus Ette went about his job of laying out preserved cadavers on the aluminium tables from the huge formalin tanks, his eyes became watery and red. Twice in the space of thirty minutes, the man had stopped and washed out his smarting eyes. A smallish man of about 60 kilograms body weight, Linus had perfected the art of lifting out the approximately 80 kilogram corpses. First, he would use a wooden plank to lift out the legs, which he would then grab with his gloved hands before using the plank as a leverage to lift out the cadaver's torso onto a nearby aluminium trolley. It would then be just a matter of rolling the cadaver on the aluminium table to complete his task. With this method, Linus was able to set out the twelve cadavers needed for the medical students anatomy demonstration class at the Lagos Southern Medical School. Then after the two-hour class, the forty-year-old mortuary attendant would have to return the bodies to the tanks to ensure proper preservation.

Less than an hour later, Linus completed the task and he stood up to stretch his back. As he peeled off the rubber gloves and apron he glanced round the mortuary and for the umpteenth time, was captivated by the beauty of the cadavers under the fluorescent lights. It was as if the bodies were actually alive only sleeping away the afternoon.

As the wall clock chimed five o'clock, the medical students started to shuffle into the room.

"Good evening, Mr Ette," the students chorused as Linus smiled and returned their greetings. After more than twenty years at the job, Linus was very popular with the students, though he sometimes envied them (for) their good clothes and carefree attitudes, which his seven children could not afford. But he secretly prayed that some of his children would one day take their place among the students.

As he sat on his stool in his partitioned cubicle, Linus observed the students as they clustered round the tables. Some of them sat down to serious work; others stood about cracking jokes and chasing each other about the room. In between answering to the students needs, Linus quietly and happily reminded himself of his six o'clock appointment. It was an appointment he had been looking forward to for a very long time. Although the details of the deal were still hazy to him, his friend James who negotiated the deal on his behalf had assured him that it would fetch him a tidy sum of money. Each time Linus remembered the appointment, a little smile would cross his face as he thought of the various things he would do with the money.

"Excuse me, Mr Ette," a voice suddenly made Linus turn round. "Somebody is asking for you outside," one of the medical students, who had got into the mortuary attendant's cubicle without his knowledge, said.

Frowning, Linus glanced at the clock. It was still half-past five, not yet time for the deal. All the same, Linus went outside into the brightness of the afternoon light, only to meet Peter, his eldest son, waiting for him.

"Papa, Mama said to ask whether Alfred and Mary are with you?"

"With me? How can they be with me? Didn't I tell them to go and wait at Uncle Sam's place from where you were to get them?"

"I - I didn't know that you told them that. I - I haven't checked Uncle Sam's place."

"You didn't check there"

No Papa, I -I -"

You must be stupid. You should have first checked there before rushing here", Linus shouted before going back to the mortuary. The silly idiot, he thought. Imagine coming all that way here instead of checking at Sam's workshop that was nearer to the house. As he returned to his post Linus glanced at the clock.

It was still twenty minutes to six and a joyous thrill went through him at the thought of what awaited him. Again he smiled. If the deal came through, he might even retire earlier than he had planned, not that he didn't like his present job; in fact, the opposite was the case, he enjoyed it. Apart from the caustic fumes of formalin, Linus did not find the job unpleasant in any way. Although once in a while the cadavers slipped from his hands and splashed back into the tank, soaking him in a spray of formalin, Linus was still happy with the job. And apart from his regular pay, there were other moneymaking opportunities that came with the job, the most lucrative being the purchase of cadavers that were mainly unclaimed corpses from traffic accidents and suicides. In the past, such corpses were very much available but now, with the reduced incidence of traffic accidents and an upsurge in the number of new medical schools in the country, corpses had become scarce, with prices as high as three thousand Naira per body. Very much in demand were cadavers of embryos, necessary for the study of embryology as well as congenital diseases including genetic errors.

Since Linus had full authority to purchase cadavers for Southern University Medical School, he made additional money from this business. He had become so skilful in buying corpses that he started reselling them to other medical schools and firms that deal in skeletons, as well as other buyers. Despite his wife's admonitions, he continued to purchase the corpses from virtually anywhere. Apart from mortuary attendants at government hospitals, Linus also purchased bodies from individuals who alleged to be selling the bodies of their dead relatives to offset debts.

"Don't ever believe anything like that," his wife had warned when he told her about this new group of suppliers. "In our culture, it is rare to find someone selling off his dead relative for whatever reason. Those people are definitely not the type you should do business with," his wife had added.

In spite of this warning, Linus expanded his business of buying and selling corpses from any source. Soon he was swamped with more requests than he could cope with. Presently, he had orders to supply ten corpses to certain people who claimed to be acting on behalf of some medical schools. In fact, the people were so desperate that they were ready to offer five thousand Naira per body and seven thousand, if the corpse was that of a baby or toddler.

Although Linus had read in the papers about unscrupulous people who were engaged in a body-selling business, Linus continued buying and selling corpses. He explained to his wife, "as long as I don't kill anybody, I have nothing to worry about. My work is just to buy and sell."

The clock soon struck six o'clock and Linus was excited. He glanced round the mortuary, happy to see that the class was still busy with Dr. Morris, the anatomy lecturer who was now going round the tables answering student's questions. Linus knew he wouldn't be missed whenever he decided to dash out for his appointment.

At a quarter past six, James peeped into the mortuary and beckoned to Linus. His heart now racing madly, Linus quietly sneaked outside to join James at the door.

"They are here already," James said, pointing to three men who stood under a mango tree near the car park.

" As I told you, this is going to be a good, honest deal so you have nothing to be afraid of", James added quickly as they walked to the men.

The discussion quickly got underway with the leader of the three men, a short stocky man with a bad left eye, explaining things to Linus. " We shall be supplying you an average of three corpses every week until you don't want anymore."

Three corpses a week? Linus smacked his lips. With that kind of supply, he would soon be able to meet the demand of his clients.

"The bodies will be supplied to you at the cost of one thousand Naira per body, payable in advance," the man added. Linus was now wild with excitement. If he bought a body at one thousand Naira and sold it at five thousand, he would make a clean profit of four thousand per body! With ten bodies that would come to forty thousand Naira! He was so engrossed in his calculations that he didn't even listen again to what the man was saying. All he did was blurt out:

"I hope I can have one or two child corpses in the consignment?"

"No sweat, my man," the one-eyed fellow answered. "In fact every consignment will contain at least one child's corpse."

"At least one child?" Linus asked breathlessly as his fevered mind made further calculations. That will fetch me a cool six thousand.

"Yes sir. Now can we have the money for the first consignment? It's getting late," the one-eyed fellow said, thrusting out his hand. Quickly, his hand trembling, Linus brought out his wallet and counted out the money. As he was about to hand the money over to the man, he shot James an anxious look.

" It is alright," James said. "You can pay them."

After counting the money, the one-eyed fellow who called himself Mr. Bello shook Linus by the hand and said, "By eight o'clock tonight, you will find three sacks by the mortuary door. They are all yours." Then the men entered a hired taxi and drove away with James.

Linus was beside himself with joy as he returned to the mortuary to finish his work for the day. And because the anatomy session dragged on till very late, it wasn't until half past seven that Linus got home. His worried-looking wife met him.

"Linus, we haven't found Alfred," She said, tears streaming down her face.

"You can't find who?" Linus asked. "How about Mary?"

"She's here. She said that Alfred decided to go to your office instead of to Uncle Sam's place. Since then we haven't seen him."

Linus was aghast! "And Sam didn't see him, either?"

"No, I even asked Peter to check his teacher's house in case he stopped there as he sometimes does." Just then Peter ran into the house breathlessly.

"Papa! Papa some of Alfred's classmates said they saw him enter a taxi with a man about an hour ago."

"A man? Which man?" Linus screamed visibly shaken.

"They said the man had a bad eye," Peter added.

"A bad what?" Linus shouted. When Peter repeated himself, Linus' mind went to his recent deal and he broke out in a cold sweat.

"Jesus, son of God! I'm finished, he said as he now looked round for a flashlight.

"Linus, what is it? Who is the man?" Mrs Ette asked but her husband was not listening. He was already half-running, half-stumbling in the direction of the medical school.

He arrived at the mortuary half an hour later and made straight for the three blood-soaked sacks lying by the door. With his penknife, he tore open the first sack, shone his flashlight inside, and then went on to the second one. His hands shook as he opened the third sack. He steeled himself opening this last sack.

As he stared at the corpse of his seven-year-old son in the sack, Linus let out an ear-shattering scream that could be heard for miles.

GODDESS OF THE STORM

By

Chukwuma Okoye-Nwajiaga

For three whole months I was plagued by unprecedented bad luck. Everything I touched seemed determined to fail, as if some unfathomable sinister influence had inserted itself into the rhythm of my life. I had never had it so bad. To think I had actually projected those months as my best. I even, for the first time in my life, made serious plans towards saving for my final disembarkation from bachelorhood. But then it began to pour without any warning lightning or thunder. First was Sidi. And then Oku. There was no single person to turn to in the end.

Sidi was my fiancée. It was together that we laid the aborted foundation for matrimony. But things suddenly went awry the very evening Sidi told me her father did not approve of me. That was not a particularly surprising piece of news, if it was news at all, for we both knew he wouldn't. He had indeed insinuated that he would rather eat pork than take a Christian for son (-in-law); and he would rather die than conceive pork in nutritional terms. And being a bohemian of sorts, one who enjoyed life as roundly as his build – he had a ravenous appetite for food, comparable only with his appetite for women – Alhaji Abdulazeez would rather die than give up the good life. This meant that he would be long dead before he would hear of a Christian son-in-law, a dreadful sacrilegious proposition that only portend a litter of pork eating grandchildren. As Allah is witness Alhaji Abdulazeez would rather give up the good life than take a Christian son-in-law. But we both knew all this. Yet we stubbornly went ahead with our plans in spite of it. Sidi confirmed she desired his blessing but would rather do without it than do without me as husband. So we conspired to commit matrimony without anybody's consent if we couldn't help it. But then Sidi sat there on my couch and told me gravely that her father did not approve of me as if she was telling me something important.

"I would break down and cry if he said otherwise," I smiled indulgently at Sidi.

"This is no smiling matter Phillip. Alhaji says he would rather eat pork than give his daughter to a pork-eater."

"In that case he can give his daughter to me without fear. I can swear over my father's grave that I have never eaten pork," I joked.

"You know what I mean Phillip. Please get serious."

"What do you mean 'get serious' Sidi? Did we not expect his disapproval? Did you not vow to marry whether or not he approved?" *This was getting rather serious,* I thought.

"I did but I never knew he would disapprove so passionately. I'm certainly not one for force-feeding him pork. Lets simply forget about this... this marriage."

"This is ridiculous Sidi." *I was beginning to lose my patience.* "What in God's name is all this?"

"In Allah's mighty name pork is an abominable meat."

"You eat pork, don't you Sidi?"

"Phillip watch out. We are speaking of Alhaji Abdulazeez not Sidi Abdulazeez." *Can you beat this? She was getting impatient with me too.*

"Well, an Abdulazeez can only beget another Abdulazeez." I muttered. *Yes, I was positively hot with malice.*

"I beg your pardon."

"If he hates pork with such saintliness why does he look like a pig?" *I shot my missile and it arrived right on target.*

"Phillip, don't insult my father, you hear?" She warned murderously.

"Oh, now I understand. Perhaps he hates pork precisely because of that. He has no obvious cannibalistic bent."

She made a hurried move to dispense one of her characteristic slaps, but I neither cringed nor made any attempt to block it. I simply smiled maliciously. She froze in mid-flight.

"You dare not Sidi. You touch me and I'll kill you," I threatened through clenched teeth.

She picked up her handbag and made for the door.

"You are an animal Phillip. I would never have married you." She was almost at the door.

"You are a pork Sidi," I shot back. "To think I would have married you."

She turned abruptly and flung her handbag at me. I made no motion to dodge or block the missile. It landed precisely on my forehead. I smiled thinly as I made my way slowly towards her. She took one look at me and saw an unfamiliar aggrieved monster with flaming red eyes and shiny white fangs, and then she fled through the door, leaving behind her handbag and her left slipper which slipped off in her haste. I had become the monster she made. She looked back to assess her safety and screamed desperately as she saw me ravenously gnawing at the slipper. The second slipper came off as she made for the safety of the nearest compound. Then I caught myself grunting like a beast as I attacked the slipper, rending the beads and the leather asunder with my fangs and my talons. Soon I reasoned like a human being and gave up the monstrous madness. I went back slowly into the room and collapsed on the couch, which still had the delicious waning warmth of Sidi's buttocks. I tried to take account and soon caught trickles of teardrops cascading down my cheeks. *Oh my God. Sidi really tore me.*

Oku was my best friend. When I acquired the saw touch (the magical capacity to turn everything I touched into dust) after Sidi's departure from my life, Oku came to my rescue. He was going on an all expense-paid trip to West Germany and had thought deeply of a way of helping me out of my financial crisis. He gave me his selfless prescription designed to better my lot, which the accursed pork had bewitched.

"Give me the money you had saved for the ill fated marriage and I'll buy you a Toyota Hiace bus from West Germany. With it, by God's grace, you'll turn your luck around and become a tycoon after at most six months of being in the transport business."

Under Oku's tutelage I attempted the mathematics of the proposal and saw myself undeniably becoming a tycoon in my sixth month in business. I began to spend my future finances right there and then: I would first buy another bus after four months; and by the sixth month I'd buy a plot of land and then resign my job in journalism. By the eight month I would acquire my third bus and...

"You see what I mean?" Oku interrupted my first ever interesting mathematics. (There was no love lost between that subject and I while I was in school.)

"Yes I see," I concurred eagerly.

And that was how I came to sweep and dry clean my bank account and empty everything into Oku's trash can; thirty thousand and five hundred Naira in all.

Oku left for West Germany and for two good weeks I plunged myself wholeheartedly into the enterprise of preparing for my impending status. Not only did I begin to go to work late; I even began to miss out days. So devoted was I to this new enterprise that my Managing Director advised me 'in my own interests' to withdraw my service and devote it religiously to whatever it was I spent company time, stationery and space multiplying, adding and subtracting. I was littering the trashcan and even the cleaner was beginning to grumble aloud. So I took my enterprise home where I devoted all my wakeful hours to it. By the end of that second week I was undoubtedly a millionaire according to my ingenious mathematical calculations. Needless to say, I was borrowing money from all possible angles and promising as much as two hundred per cent interest, just so I could keep body and soul intact to execute my engaging calculations. So engrossed was I that I hardly took notice of the news of Sidi's wedding to an obscure millionaire in Lagos. *I was also on my way there*, I told myself confidently.

Then I got the shocking news that Oku was somewhere in Lagos squandering his new ingeniously gotten wealth. *Oh no, not Oku*, was all I could mutter before I passed out. I came to an hour and three buckets of my neighbour's water later. He made sure I recorded that down as additional debt, not forgetting the usual two-hundred-percent interest. According to his own mathematical calculations he was owed six hundred Naira and nine buckets of clean water from the famous local tanker driver. My mathematical naivety returned when I tried to calculate my total debt in water and money and arrived at unbelievably outrageous summations. I decided there and then that I had to leave, run away, perhaps for only a while, before I took to the market in advanced madness. I simply had to get away from there or endanger my sanity.

All through the night of the eve of my exile, as I called it, I lay awake and tried, without (understandably) venturing into mathematics or any such figural nightmare, to rationalise my condition. It was in this sober mien that I, a civilised freethinker, began to see clearly the unmistakable evil remote hands of my enemies at work. I discovered there and then that something, if not someone was apparently behind my catalogue of ill luck. *Or how else could I rationalise all this?* And being one who can hardly tell APC from Panadol, how much more know the metaphysical antidote for the evil remote machinations of my enemies, I strongly resolved to hide for sometime. Perhaps when they miss me they'll turn my luck around and find other victims for my misfortune.

It was in this state that I remembered Seye, my best friend at school, who was then teaching at the College of Education in Oyo. He was my true best friend, not the type that Oku was. Seye would never lie to me, much more squander my marriage savings, despite the fact that the marriage was never going to take place now. Seye would not. *Tomorrow morning, just before dawn, I would sneak out of my compound and leave for Oyo,* I conspired with myself.

Just as I'd planned, even before Prophet Mohammed's votary began his irritating electronically amplified drawl, **Allahu-ak-**blarring the ungrateful neighbourhood of infidels into premature wakefulness, I was up and gone. I had packed my bag with only a few clothes, but I took all the money I had left, which added up to quite a sum considering I was woefully in debt. I was going to enjoy myself, if I could work myself up to it.

After all there was no hope in my mind. I would simply chill out for a while and then possibly proceed to my parents'.

In the bus I worked out my story for Seye - in the early hours crammed tightly between generous doses of sleep. I would tell him everything or nothing, depending on the nature of his reception. I mean I would either tell him the whole truth or the whole lie – without the suspicious metaphysical insinuations of course. It wouldn't do to make myself look ridiculous before an old friend of mine.

"Good morning to you all in the Almighty name of Jesus Christ..." a feminine voice trumpeted into my right ear. Emerging abruptly from my slumber I reached desperately to block out the irritating aural sensation from my ear and unwittingly slapped the luscious full lips of the pretty diminutive girl in the colourful headscarf that sat to my right. Her spectacles and Bible flew off. I juggled with them precariously and was only barely able to catch the spectacles just as they hit the floor. I picked the Bible from under the seat and meekly offered them to her with profuse apologies. While I wrestled with the Bible and the spectacles some mischievous boys behind us laughed uproariously.

"I am very sorry please," I stammered.

"You are a demon," she observed as she unceremoniously snatched her appurtenances from my hands. *How clairvoyant*. Only at the time I was only the victim of a demon, I thought.

"Ah, our sister in Christ sorry o. Come see as dis brother don shurup your mout in the Almighty name of Jesus Christ," one of the boys sympathised amidst derisive laughter.

"Na your mama wey born you na im mout e shurup, you accursed demonic children. God go *soda una yansh*," she cursed piously.

"Abi your own God na blacksmith?" another boy enquired.

"Na your mama be blacksmith; Na your papa..." She was going to go on and empty her devout missiles on these unfortunate boys' derisive heads when a respectable looking gentleman in the rear came to their rescue. Indeed to the rescue of all of us.

"Young lady such demonic curses should not come into the head of a Christian, how much more through her lips," the man said with vocal timbre that only derived from long years at the pulpit. Everyone was silent. The cheery boys shrank into their ill-fitting school uniforms, while our sister-in-Christ buried her head in shame. Only her stubborn spectacles remained intransigent.

Such was the mood in which we got to Owode Park in Oyo. While everyone scrambled to collect his or her baggage from the back of the bus the reverend gentleman stood a strategic ground and, obviously encouraged by the effect of his voice on the passengers, placed his left palm against his right breast, stretched out his hand in a fashion that belonged undeniably to the Vatican, and proceeded to dispense unsolicited blessings to each one in turn.

"May the peace of the Lord be with you" he said to me when it was my turn.

"Thank you ehm..." I almost said Pope. I escaped as fast as I could and went in search of an English – speaking taxi driver who would get me to my destination. I found one soon enough and was in the college compound in no time at all. Seye must be a very popular teacher with the students – with the female folks at least – for the very first girl I met twitched with embarrassing anxiety.

"Oh, Uncle Seye... he has gone home. I know his house so I can take you there if you wish," she offered pleasantly.   As she led the way I lustfully engaged in the enthralling puzzle of deciphering the delicate rhythm of her bewitching buttocks. There was something osmotic about them, for no matter how hard I tried I could not yank my soul from them.   Soon my heartbeat began to orchestrate this rhythm as my mind transported me somewhere else, even as I followed her. Almost with a mind of its own, certain delicious warmth began to course through my bowels.

"That is Uncle Seye's house," she pointed.

I collided against those buttocks in my reverie. I tried to stammer apologies but she only displayed a knowing smile as she picked up my bag from the floor and offered it to me charmingly.

"That is Uncle Seye's house", she pointed out again. I followed her fingers backwards and ended in the bodacious firmness of her... *No!* I tore my eyes away from those tortuous mounds.

"Thank you very much," I stammered.

"You are welcome – anytime," she smiled, threw me a coquettish look and swiftly took up the rhythm of the bewitching buttocks. *Phillip what's the matter with you?* I rebuked myself with a hard knock to the head. I contorted my face as I tried to soothe the self – inflicted pain with my palm. She looked back and arrested me in that obnoxious posture. For a second the world stood still. Then she set the spheres back in motion again and released me with a rippling laugh. I hurriedly took the stairs to Seye's apartment and began to press feverishly on the doorbell. The door swung in swiftly and Seye appeared angrily.

"What's the matter with you, are you...? Oh my God, its you Phillip! He exclaimed happily.

"Yes its me I assured him.

"Come on in; come on in," he hurried me into the sitting room and gave me a most endearing bear hug.   We both collapsed on the couch with cheery laughter.

"I can't believe this, Phillip," he exclaimed.

Well after all the pleasantries and expressions of delightful surprise had been exchanged Seye informed me that he would be leaving for Lagos in the evening on an official assignment. He would be back by noon the next day.

"How long are you staying?" he asked.

"Just a couple of days." I lied.

The time was not yet ripe for my tale of woe. He offered me a drink and we generally tried to catch up on all gossip.

Later that evening Seye left for Lagos with a promise to be back by noon the following day. I lay in bed for the greater part of the evening, reading a rather uninteresting novel.   Occasionally the image of my aide's rhythmic buttocks would assail my imagination. Then the delightful warmth would spread again.   At those thoughts I would squeeze my thighs together and let out a soft moan.   Later when it was getting dark I decided to go out for a walk and maybe call at the bar I had seen opposite the school compound for a beer or two.

I got up from the bed and stepped into the bosom of the cool night. I felt positively elated and recklessly free. All my troubles seemed so far away, further away than the distance between Ibadan and Oyo. I had no single worry in the whole world. I unconsciously executed a quick happy caper under a street lamp and immediately looked around to ensure I had no audience.

There was none that I could see; though I felt there was one I couldn't see.   I became rather uncomfortable and embarrassed so I quickened my steps to the bar. I took the table in the left extreme of the surprisingly comfortable and neat bar and ordered a bottle of Star beer, which was promptly delivered by a clever looking young attendant. The bar was immersed in the cool blue light of an overhead lamp. Save for a group of men sitting round a table near the counter the bar was conveniently empty. This group must have been there for quite some time, for though there were no visible victims of their revelry standing on the table or anywhere else – obviously a statement of the attendant's efficiency – their voices sounded unusually boisterous and passionate.

"Did you see it with your own eyes?" queried one of the voices.

"So what? So what if I did not see it with my eyes then I have no reason to believe it?" Replied another harshly.

"Seeing is believing," pronounced the sage amongst them. "Shut up you bloody fool!" ordered another impatiently.

"Facking you," cursed the sage.

"Your Mama…"

"Will you shut up and let us hear word!" ordered one of the voices exasperatedly. "We are talking sense, you are talking nonsense the two of you."

"All I wan' know is whether you saw it with your own eyes."

"I didn't, but somebody who is very reliable did and told me"

"Who?"

"Let me tell you, my mother told me that my father told her that he was there when it happened, and he saw everything with his own two eyes."

"Then your mother is a liar. Your father is a liar. That's why they gave birth to a voracious liar like you. In fact, your whole family –"

"It's your Mama who is a liar. Your Papa..." as he got up angrily the table jerked and they all began a desperate battle to save their drinks from spilling. Miraculously not one bottle got broken and not much of their drinks spilled. As the voices rose in unreserved assault of the unfortunate culprit there came a power failure. Everyone chorused "*NEPA!*"

"You see what you have caused? The two of you. You see? Now you have gone and annoyed NEPA," complained the sage in the sudden darkness.

"Shut up you bloody drunkard."

"Facking you."

"Your mama..."

"Yee! Who owns this hand? Chei! Somebody is taking away my beer! Put on your candle or lamp barman."

"There's no kerosene"

I felt a movement beside me and immediately snatched my bottle of beer from the table. After about two minutes of darkness, the light came on to reveal one of the querulous voices sitting at another table. He had apparently transferred under the cover of darkness to guarantee the safety of his beer. There he was now, clutching the bottle possessively to his chest. He smiled cunningly and proceeded to join the others again. Just then I beheld a most amazing sight. Sitting directly opposite me, three tables away, was the most beautiful woman I had ever seen. She looked positively out of place in this dim bar. Even the voices were momentarily silenced in awe. Our eyes met and held for a couple of seconds. Then she smiled a coy smile and I smiled an embarrassed reply. She got up and walked elegantly to my table, trailed slavishly by the more-than-a-dozen bewildered eyes of the drunken voices.

"May I?" she asked, indicating the empty chair before me.

"Yes please," I uttered nervously as I struggled awkwardly to stand up without knocking the table over.

"Thanks," she said graciously as she took the chair and sat down.

"You are welcome"

I sat down and immediately began to experience familiar warm stirrings. Her gait was clearly reminiscent of my aide's rhythmic buttocks. She felt familiar in fashion that was not physical; for she was unlike any lady I had ever seen. Yet as she smiled elegantly I had an overpowering feeling of déjà vu.

"You are new around here, aren't you?" she asked.

"Yes. In fact this is my first time here, how did you guess?"

"I didn't guess, I know."

"How?" I insisted good-naturedly.

"Well, anyone who bothers can read you like a book in the library. Let me say that like the chicken in a strange land you are standing on one foot only." And then she smiled that coy smile again. As if she said "you know what I mean." But I honestly didn't.

"I didn't know I am that legible," I replied, feeling gradually more at ease in her company.

In my pre-occupation with this enthralling company I no longer took notice of the voices. I was surprised to look up and find them leaving in assorted drunken gaits. Soon there was just me and the beautiful young lady left in the whole bar, and of course the efficient waiter who sat inattentively behind the counter. I ordered a bottle of beer or any other drink of her choice for her, but she declined and requested a glass of water instead.

"What is your name?"

She smiled and shook her head gently from side to side in a gesture of refusal.

"Naturally I know you would want to know, but don't get ideas just because I came to your table uninvited."

"I am sorry, but..." I stammered as I tried to disguise my ideas."

"Well, just to warn you. Anyway, I'll tell you later when we meet again," she said with that smile. "Now you can tell me about yourself."

Without an iota of restraint I began to tell this strange adorable lady my life history, especially my tale of many woes. She was a most sympathetic and avid listener. Looking at her, the expression on her face, one felt like talking the whole world through. I was so relaxed in her company. It must have had something to do with her, although I must admit that with three bottles of beer in the head the tongue was bound to be loose. I talked my entire life away. I told her of Oku; and of Sidi; and of Seye, and of everything. It was a very long monologue. Then all of a sudden she glanced at her wristwatch and stood up.

"It's so late. I'm sorry I have to run along," she said as she began to leave.

"Hold on, let me finish my drink and see you off," I offered.

"No don't bother. I like walking on my own. Besides I can't wait a second longer."

"So how shall we see again... tomorrow perhaps?" I threw in hurriedly just as she arrived at the door. She stopped and looked at me with that smile again.

"Well, I'll meet you again, certainly."
"When?"
"When I want"
"Can't we make it...?"

She was gone. I hurriedly downed my beer in three desperate gulps, over-paid the waiter because there was no time to wait for my change, and rushed into the quiet street. She was nowhere to be found. Street lamps lighted the entire road to the left and to the right yet she was nowhere visible. I wondered at that briefly and simply dismissed it. Then I began to walk light headed for Seye's apartment. I was moderately drunk and on top of the world. I carried her gloriously amazing presence in my head all the way. The night was beginning to get cloudy and stormy, but I simply walked on like a king of the road.

When I got to Seye's place I went straight to bed, but for a long time I could not sleep. The persistent images of these two girls I had encountered merged into one intense whole and plagued my longing. My desire was becoming unbearable. I closed my eyes and moaned softly. Outside I heard the gathering storm whooping intently. My desire allied with the spirit and the soul of the storm and then it became more violent. It must have gathered into a tornado for I heard the bellowing sound whirling around the house. As my longing intensified I began to feel a little light-headed.... Dreamy.... Weightless; and as the tornado fused with my longing I began to develop an erection...distanced. Then purposefully the tornado broke into the room and began to twirl viciously like a dancing *egungun* masquerade. Yet the windows and door remained securely locked. The tornado simply passed through them. Then it began to contract into a decipherable spiral in the middle of the room, before my bed. As it contracted a human figure slowly began to take shape within it. While the figure grew more and more definite the spiral began to disintegrate. Then I saw her draped in black cotton cloth with the sheer transparency of organza and the glossy suppleness of satin. With the cloth loosely clinging to her body enveloped in the soft dying spiralling wind she became a black billowing wave. Under the wrap she was savagely provocative. I was in the presence of a most brutal sexuality and my penis acknowledged with an unprecedented turgidity, pointing in stiff shameless appraisal of her voluptuous half-nakedness like a shotgun. Her eyes were bright, fiery, hungry, savage, but yet soft and alluring. Her face had the austere sharpness and lustre of an African sculpture complete with thick black braided coiffure. And she had the now familiar hint of a smile. Her sensuous breasts were harshly defined by the loose cotton into two proud mounds with two crystal-hard nipples pointing audaciously at diagonals to each other. She was everything. Then she viciously tore the black cloth down the middle in one swift motion and revealed her most exquisite nakedness. Her body was jet-black and her skin shone like polished china. It was captivatingly luminous. Around her waist and neck were strings of brown glass beads interspersed with pink and white coral beads. These had an affecting presence of their own, exuding an irresistible sensuous luminosity against the background of her ebony blackness. She let the two pieces of cloth float delicately free of her fingers. As they fell to her sides they quickly melted on the floor into two receding sea waves. Then she stood there, proud and naked, a faultlessly sculpted sensuous African statue in ebony. And she smiled that murderously cunning smile as she slowly tore the beads from her body, string by string. A turbulent storm began to rage inside me, coursing through my senses and threatening to break out into countless shreds. I was in the eye of a whirlpool of passion. All of a sudden her eyes assumed a severe ferocity. She began to grunt like an enraged buffalo. In one flash she tore my clothes away from my body, revealing my penis in all its turgid fidelity. Then she began to tear me apart with deft savagery. I watched helplessly as she tore out my pulsating heart, my abdomen and my trailing intestines and scattered them all into the floating essences. Yet I felt no pain. I longed for more. It was heavenly. The river within me coursed more riotously. I watched, urging her, pleading silently, and sacrificing myself like a votary on the altar of savage sensuality. She grasped the shaft of my erection with her brutal talons and yanked it out furiously like a cassava stem, tubers and roots. The raging river within gushed out triumphantly through my groin, trailing the tubers and the roots of my shaft, dripping an obscene slimy liquid, which convulsed into a snaky river. The river within me coursed more riotously. I watched, urging her, pleading silently, and sacrificing myself like a votary on the altar of savage sensuality. She grasped the shaft of my erection with her brutal talons and yanked it out furiously like a cassava stem, tubers and roots. The raging river within gushed out triumphantly through my groin, trailing the tubers and the roots of my shaft, dripping an obscene slimy liquid, which convulsed into a snaky river. She emitted an erotic moan as she began to draw the snaky river into her bowel. A ravenous fire burned in her eyes as she welcomed the river into her by a powerful suction. Then the river turned crimson with the hue of palm oil. As she drained the river into her storm the raging fire began to ebb, emitting simmering whispers and a hale of steam as of cool water pouring over red-hot rock. Gently the steam and the whispers died out. She smiled at me. She was satiated.

"My name is Oya"

Then she swiftly began to twirl round and round and soon became one with a viciously whirling masquerade, a spiralling tornado. She melted into this cyclonic wind, which twirled provocatively for a while and then broke out of the room as easily as it had broken in. I heard the sound outside as it journeyed home to the Niger.

As the last sound of the storm faded away I woke up with a start, sweating profusely in the delicious coolness of the night. There was dead quietness around me, but for my heart with its hurried beating. There was the unmistakable familiar tingling warmth of the dying embers of a burned -out luscious fire. *It must have been one of those dreams*, I sighed.

But did I really fall asleep? *Certainly no. I was wide-awake. I saw her concretely.* I could still smell the dying warmth of her passion in the air, her steam and palm oil. I looked around and I saw a curious bundle in the spot where she must have stood. I peered closer in the semi-darkness and what I saw immediately shook me. I began to tremble. Right there where she had stood was the greatest pile of brand new currency notes I had ever seen, carefully packed and stacked.

As the rhythm of my heartbeat changed and dawn began to break I remembered that she had indeed promised to tell me her name when we last met.

FREE TO BE ME

By

Kolapo Oyefeso

No! It isn't my fault. It can't be. Or is it? Did I somehow do something that's made me this way? Is there something wrong with me, like, from birth? Was I dropped on my head, rearranging my genes, screwing up my hormones? I don't know. I don't know! It's nobody's fault. It just is. Yeah. Believe.

I can't even tell anyone. No one here would understand. And they would crucify me behind my back. I want to but I can't. I did once, keeping it in the family, and... Poor Dad. Guess his shock and dismay at how we all turned out sent him to an early grave. There I was talking, opening up to him, bravely baring my soul and he didn't say a word. It was difficult. Very difficult. It was like talking into a black hole. I couldn't tell if he understood what I was saying. Knowing what he felt about it was out of the question. When I stopped talking and waited for him to say something – shout, curse, disown me like he did Chuks, anything – he just looked through me. Those beetling eyes with thick grey-black eyebrows stared into the space of my being. Less than a year later he was dead. Deader than all the patients who died on his table. Dead as a doornail... do doornails die? Guess they do. Anything gets hit on the head hard like that should die. Dad definitely died. He looked like a slab of dark grey putty. A well-dressed slab, as distant in death as in life. And I killed him. We killed him.

All his children but one (disappointments all. Not one living up to or even getting anywhere near his expectations) stood by his grave and watched the earth fall on him. Chuks wasn't at the funeral. Dad disowned him long before then (until he did it I thought being disowned was something that happened only in books, like 'go / and darken my doorstep no more'. My brother is the only person I know in the world who has been disowned). He wasn't at the funeral, but when the will was to be read he turned up. I don't blame him. When the will was read I was amazed. I knew Dad was rich but had no idea how much he had. There really was a lot of stuff to share. Chuks tried to pull some first-son shit but it didn't go; the will had a clause for everything he could think of. Now he's another problem lingering on my mind. With Chuks disowned and non-existent as far as the will is concerned, I am the oldest son; the trustees ask me before they do anything. The snag is Mum. Ever since I told her, opening up to her like I did with Dad, she's gone off me. I don't blame her. It's hard for me to believe I am not abnormal. When I told her she said, 'I don't believe,' in a soft voice. Then she screamed it, as if trying to convince herself, and she hasn't said anything about it since then. To her, not believing a thing must mean that thing does not exist. We talk and all now, but there's a distance between us: an edge to her voice, wariness in the corners of her eyes. With Chuks she's different. He's her first son who's been done wrong. She says his being disowned wasn't his fault. I can't see how it wasn't. A man gambles away the school fees and allowances of his siblings, leaving them to fend as best they can, in a cold, friendless foreign land, with Dad back at home thinking we were okay, till he got a telegram:

Dear Dad,
No money. Cold and hungry. Out of school.

Help!

Abi and Reni

Reni wrote the telegram. I remember telling her to put 'out of school' before 'cold and hungry' because I was sure Dad wouldn't give a shit if we were dying of cold and hunger as long as we were in school – that's what I thought of him then. Mum says it wasn't Chuks' fault. Maybe she's right. Maybe it was Dad's fault for trusting him with so much money.

I am tired of living a lie. Hiding things, dodging, disappearing for hours when I can't hold myself back, when my need gets too much for me. Seeking relief in dark dingy places with strangers that pass, afraid, drinking hard to numb my fear and guilt, and going back home happy and sad. Sated yet dreading, and anticipating, the next time. I understand myself better now, thank God. I have stopped looking for where to place the blame or, more to the truth, places to share it out. Gave some to my father for not loving me and for being such a cold fish; a bit to Mum for not letting him love his children – how did she do this? I don't know, but she did, or didn't do, something. Some – a good bit actually – to the school in England where it all started. A prison-like public school. 400 boys with about a million rules to share between them. You would think with such a regulated life, everyone would turn out straight and narrow but it was the reverse. The rules were on the surface. A totally different existence went on beneath that cover. The teachers knew but as long as fees were paid, their eyes, same as the rules, were kept on the surface. Not all of them though, some joined in the fun. The leftover blame, I kept for me.

I don't believe anyone is to blame any longer. I blamed me so much I once tried to end it all – just once; I wasn't very good at it, haha. To stop the voice that was making my life so miserable. I get the shivers now thinking about it. Days of dwelling on soft, painless ways to do it ended in a bottle of aspirin washed down with gin. Aspirin and gin met all my conditions: no sharp or cruel implements; no blood; no pain (didn't know anything then); reversible (hindsight. Though I remember thinking about stomach pumps at some point); cheap because I didn't have the money I have now, then. The gin seemed sort of fitting, celebratory, sort of a good way to go. I lifted that from under Dad's lock and key. I didn't die but, Jesus! The pain. It cleared my mind, driving all other thoughts away. All I wanted was for it to stop so I dragged myself to the hospital. The doctor later said that, another hour and my stomach would have been perforated. I suppose... no, I know I didn't really want to die. I could have used Valium or rat poison or something. Reading about suicide afterwards, I figured that what I wanted was:

        a) Attention or
        b) Punishment or
        c) Both

I got both and more. I got attention from my family, which led to my having to see a psychiatrist because when I told Dad why I did it, he stared through me. Mum refused to believe. I was judged as mad. Not very mad but mad enough to need a brain doctor. My punishment was short and sharp and illuminating. I hate myself. I am a failure. The only good thing that happened, at least it seemed like that at the time, was that I met my wife.

It's really Chinye I should tell. God knows I've given her all sorts of hints and clues, and I know she's not daft. She must know, or suspect. Things have changed so much between us. We hardly ever talk these days; I mean real talk like we used to. These days it's, 'Will you pick the children up from school?' 'I've paid the bills.' 'Your food is in the oven.' Meaningless politeness, avoiding quarrels, skirting issues, not wanting to damage the children the way my parents did me. Tosan and Tolani, I often tell myself, are the reason I am living this lie; now I am not so sure I am doing them any good. For them Chinye and I act out a marriage but I think they know something is wrong. Sometimes Tolani climbs onto my lap and stares into my face like she's looking for something and when I ask her what; she shakes her head and gets down. Tosan has a worried look when he thinks no one is looking. He's six years old. The cycle starts again. I must stop it. I must tell Chinye, and whatever comes of it, comes.

The first time I saw Chinye, I was lying on my back watching a mixture of normal saline and glucose drip into my life. Drop after drop after drop. It was my third day in hospital after my aspirin and gin cocktail. I couldn't eat – doctor's orders so my stomach would heal – and survived on intravenous fluids. The pain had stopped and I had lost the clarity of mind induced by my agony. Once again my mind was filled with the usual clutter, only, now, the clutter had a faint, flickering purplish edge. I was now afraid of myself. My survival instinct is not as strong as my self-destructiveness. I watched the drops to escape.

I saw Reni first. You can't help but see her, my little sister. Everyone in the ward saw her. Heads turned to follow her. The man several beds from me, who had been groaning and calling, 'Nurse-o nurse-o' a few minutes earlier, stared at her. Hair several hues, black lipstick, tight blouse and mini-skirt, Reni strode through the ward like some sort of cross between a model and a gladiator and my spirits soared. She dresses for effect, my little sister, but she never looks cheap. Her clothes were well cut, obviously designer-labels and her make up was faultless. That she looked weird was in her eyes, weird and hard. A no-nonsense chick.

Chinye was with her – not that I knew who she was then – and I liked her immediately. It was more than that. I actually felt a sexual attraction. Relief, and a sense of freedom, overcame me. Maybe the a. & g. cocktail that failed to kill me had reversed my hormones. The last time I truly noticed a girl was when I was twelve and now there was this slim light-skinned girl with high cheekbones and grey-green eyes stirring me. She was Reni's friend from school now in Lagos looking for work. We got on very well right from the start, and I, trying to get away from my difference, trying very hard to be normal, pursued her relentlessly. In between bullshitting my brain doctor and avoiding my parents, I went after Chinye, clinging to her like a drowning man, my lifeline to a regular, acceptable existence. The first time I made love to her was an event. To hold down my nervousness, I had a strong drink covertly topped with some grass. I played my music, my tongue danced wittily and we laughed and loved. My relief when I found I could do it, when I did do it – even though I kept bending her gender in my mind while at it, which wasn't difficult, she was so slim – was so great that I asked her to marry me.

Dad was dead by then, Mum was so relieved, every one was thrilled, I was afraid. Because my hormones were now going flip-flop, and I was caught in between. We got married and the lies, the vague having to see someone for something, started. It started slowly. I didn't need to see my friends often and it seemed as if I could make it work, burn both ends, have and eat cake. Then Tosan came. I was a father. Suddenly I was playing so many roles I got confused. The only time I felt safe was when I was on my own. Chinye put on a lot of weight and I couldn't get it up for her anymore. Not even fantasizing helped. I bought some blue movies to play while screwing and this helped a bit. Then Tolani came and it all got worse. Chinye now weighed three times what she did when I first saw her. Our sex life, or lack of one, became a big thing. I dropped hints, got calls from men that she didn't know, disappeared for days, and we stopped talking.

I don't know why I haven't been able to tell her, to really come out and say it instead of hoping she'll see what's staring her in the face and do something about it. We haven't made love in almost two years. Sometimes I want to tell her she should find a boyfriend but that's dangerous ground, that's divorce territory and I don't want that. Besides, I am not sure how I'll feel if she does. After all, she's still my wife and in some strange twisted way, I love her.

I am what I am. I have come to accept this but how do I tell Chinye that I prefer boys to girls? How? Because, see, I want to be free.

PLEATED SKIRTS
(For Kunle who knows why)

By

Harry Garuba

She woke up at the crack of dawn, before the alarm
clock at her bedside rang. She had diligently set the
alarm the night before to wake her up at 4a.m because
she had had so many sleepless nights of late that she
could no longer trust the sharpness of her senses. Her
reflexes, once so dependable, had become a shadow of
what they used to be. In her waking moments, she often
found herself drifting off into reveries of vengeance and
blood so curdling that she was shocked at the
vehemence of her anger and wondered at the depth of
hurt that had lodged this violence in her soul. At sleep
the nightmares refused to leave and she would dream
of slaughterhouses and carnage that would shame all
but the most dedicated bloodhound. And these would
go on without unceasingly for most of the night. So she
could no longer sleep at night and had taken to staying
awake all-night and sleeping just before the crack of
dawn.

Last night, she had willed herself to sleep by continually
suggesting to her mind that she had to wake up early to
visit her husband in jail. The military dictator had
detained Kunle -her husband - because he was the
editor of a newspaper that had dared publish the story
of an attempted putsch against the general. The story

written by a colleague of his had been so accurate in every material particular, as they say, that the general had been justifiably infuriated. He didn't mind journalists publishing falsehoods and he had become so used to the speculation and rumours; the half-truths, and the crazily off the mark reports that he had come to like them and now took delight in having them read to him. But this piece had hit him where it hurt: not only was it true, it also contained the names of some of his closest associates who had taken part in the plot. Although he knew that they had been behind the failed coup, he had wanted to keep the knowledge a secret to keep them guessing: he had wanted to watch them as he always did, to play with them the way a cat teases a cornered mouse. He loved the alternation of despair and fawning that this occasioned, the god-like power it conferred on him. The last time this had happened, he'd waited, biding his time. For two weeks he had played the game with General Ibrahim, summoning him to his office everyday, at odd hours of day and night, to watch him cower and kow-tow, tell on his best friends, rat on his lieutenants and betray every one he could. Now he had lost that power just because of a bloody reporter.

So he was justifiably angry this time around, infuriated that this two-bit journalist who had no idea of the pleasures of power had undercut him and denied him the sweetest joy of all. He had sent soldiers to deal with the bloody civilian journalist, ordering them through his aide-de-camp to make sure that they picked up the right man not the editor or some other top functionary, the right one, the idiot who really wrote the story. He must not be allowed to slip out of the country. When the security forces came to the newspaper offices, they had simply picked her husband up without making any charges or offering any explanations. The Judas who was supposed to identify the writer with a kiss had been wrong-footed by Kunle who rushed forward and, with a flourish, kissed her on the cheeks. Kunle had no idea what was going on. He was simply in a teasing flirtatious mood that morning. As he often did on such occasions, he looked at the young man beside the svelte lady and said: 'sorry buddy, this lady is mine. I even paid her to get herself a chaperon. I hope she hasn't been short-changing you on that score.' The young woman tried to break away from him but he was having none of that.

'No, no, no,' he continued. 'I am not having any of that today. The secret is out!'

And, too late, he saw the look on the man's face.

When, several months later, they arraigned him before the military tribunal on charges of sedition and subversion, treason and conspiring to overthrow the government of the federal republic, they addressed him as Mr. Olu, the name of the journalist who had actually written the story. He politely reminded the court again, as he had done in the many months he had spent in detention without trial, that his name was Kunle not Olu and that they had the wrong man. For a minute the judge was nonplussed and after conferring with the prosecution had the case adjourned. At the next sitting of the court the charge sheet had been altered and his real name appeared on it but the charges remained the same. The slight error about names had been corrected and the trial began. The circus clown of a prosecutor proceeded with the farce in the spirit of comic drama by referring to the earlier confusion of names and identities as a Shakespearean instance of convoluted plotting and the audience roared in laughter while the judge noted his way with words, his punning reference to fictional plots and conspiratorial plots. In spite of himself, Kunle could not help smiling as he observed the proceedings wondering at the supreme irony of it all. And why shouldn't he? It was his life on the line and if anyone had a right to be amused it was he. And, anyway, he had already sent word to Olu to disappear from the country for his own good. And he had.

However, this morning, these were not the thoughts on Lola's mind. All she was preoccupied with was her visit to the Jos prison to see her husband. This time, for the first time, she was taking her little baby, born when Kunle had already been sentenced to fifteen years in prison. It was a special day for her because she had spent several months coaching the little boy to say Daddy. Everyday she would put an enlarged photograph of Kunle before the boy and pointing at the clean shaven face would say, 'Daddy.' The boy, squealing with laughter, would repeat the two syllables: 'Da Da.' He enjoyed the game and enthusiastically joined in every day his mother brought out the picture. But then, after several months, it became monotonous and he grew tired of it. He wondered if that was the only game that his mummy enjoyed because he could always see the glint of joy on her face whenever they played this game. Any time he saw her in a sad mood, he would go for the picture and, sticking his forefinger into the face, would say 'Da Da, Da Da, Da Da,' swaying to the singsong rhythm of the syllables. Then she would smile and pick him up in an embrace of joy.

Every time she did this, she would remember how, that night in the maternity ward, she had brought forth this miracle, her bundle of joy, which had arrived in a flood of blood as torrential as the Niger. She would remember how, like a stuck pig, she had bled with such fury that the doctors and midwives had given her up for dead.

And, yes, as the blood flowed, she had felt life ebbing away from her, slowly like a reel of still images she saw a child in a foetus of clouds unwinding gradually, the child struggling to come out and the infinite spool of clouds uncoiling slowly like blue bandages through which the baby tumbled endlessly. The vision was so clear even though she knew that she was no longer of this world; it was an out-of-body experience unfolding with the certainty of reality. As she lay helplessly there on the bed while the heavens fought to take her child, she knew that she only had to say the word of life to make the baby live. But the words eluded her, and the words teased her tongue with a sound that refused to come: she lay empty, drained of all sound, of the blood-forming words she needed for her child's life. Like a winded balloon, the cloud billows which cradled her baby were punctured by several diabolical needles and threads of smoke shot out in jets and an unbridled baby descended from the clouds in a free fall so fast it took her breath away. She tried to stretch out her hands to the fleeing baby, to reach out to let it know that it was loved and wanted, that it only had to stop if only for a moment and feel the touch of human hands, the kiss and caress of mothering lips...

And meanwhile the midwives watched the mother's limbs go limp; they saw her lose the strength to push. It never stopped amazing them, the foolishness of this woman who had insisted on a natural birth in spite of all the odds; this woman who had been brought in bleeding and still stubbornly fixated on the idea of a natural birth. You should have heard her saying it - 'I have to do it. I have to do it if only for my husband' – as if she was the only one in the world with a husband in jail. Even as her lips trembled and beads of sweat broke out on her brow, she kept saying it, intoning it like a mantra. The things women go through for their husbands! Now she had put them in this impossible situation. Couldn't she have considered the child's life even if she was so willing to throw hers away on account of her jailed husband? And these good for nothing husbands, he probably never gave a thought to his wife when he foolishly went about reporting the details of the coup. The frustration and anger were evident on the faces of the midwives. Only the doctor kept his calm. In his many years in this profession, he had learned to respect his patients' wishes because it was only then that they summoned the courage to fight when the crunch came. To him, the patients' beliefs were sacred and he only violated them in extreme situations and even then he took great care in his timing of when. Now he wondered if this was one such instance. At what point should he over ride her wishes?

But just then, as these thoughts took form in his mind, miraculously, once again, like water through a dam the blood burst, this time thrusting the baby out with the power of a pump. And, you should have heard the sighs of relief; the breath, long held, finally released in a collective exhalation of unbelief. The midwives signed the cross and the doctor was relieved that he would not, after all have to make that uncomfortable decision.

But Lola was far, far away from these mundane concerns, she saw only a blurred figure stretch out its hands and catch the child just before it hit the ground. The arms, so familiar, so tender and loving, reminded her of someone in the distant past who had held her in just the same way, had cradled her head with fingers which emitted currents of electricity and sent her into breathless ecstasies from which she feared she would never awake...and now the outline of the face was taking shape, the features were becoming distinct, the curve of the lips, the shine of the brows, the arrested fall of the nose, and the eyes so...O Kunle, she moaned, trying to stretch out her hands and that was the last she knew...until she woke up two weeks later.

She awoke at the crack of dawn, just before the alarm clock at her bedside went off. It was still dark so she had to find her way with her hands stretched out in front like a blind man's cane. For one moment she bumped into an object, which she later recognised as a suitcase. Now she had to be careful not to wake the baby. She was weaving her way round the suitcase when the alarm suddenly went off and she jumped in panic. She ran to the clock and stopped the deafening noise. Then she tiptoed to the baby and was relieved to find that he was still asleep. Now she had to find the slip of paper on which she had listed all the things she needed to do this morning before setting out. Her mother – bless her soul – had taught her to do this every time she had an important assignment to take care of. 'Write down everything, step by step,' she had told her, 'otherwise you will get where you are going only to find out that you left the most important thing behind or that you forgot to wear your bra.' And, was she fond of forgetting such things? She might as well have been a boy! As a little girl, she loved to play with the boys and quite often forgot the girl-things, which her mother always insisted upon. She would sit with her legs apart like a boy, climb trees, play street soccer and, because she was short-tempered, get into fights with bigger boys from which she came back bloodied and bruised but triumphant. It was after one such fight that her mother bought her, her first pleated skirts. In the solitude of that cold night, with the baby asleep in the cradle and the alarm clock finally disabled, she recalled from memory the lesson her mother had taught her when she had bought those pleated skirts. Mama was a primary school teacher and had cultivated the teaching habit of speaking to her children as if they were just a bunch of school kids who needed to be lectured on everything under the sky.

'As a girl, you will find this useful since you are always getting into fights and you never have the time to do things in an orderly manner.'

She stared at her mother wondering what this was all about until she'd produced this skirt from her bag. The skirt appeared all creased up and in need of ironing. That was the effect the mother had wanted to create since she knew that her little girl had never seen such a skirt in her life. She held the skirt spread out in her two hands, between forefinger and thumb, and Lola saw, for the first time in her life, a skirt so carefully creased it seemed to have been deliberately ruined. Her first reaction was 'O my God, I hope I don't have to iron that!'

And that again was what Mama wanted: to make her learn the care and attention that went into this business of being a woman by ironing this skirt, pleat after pleat, singly and properly enfolded until the last pleat was done and the skirt was ready to be adorned. It was the worst imposition of her youth and by the time she finished the ironing she had developed two little buds on her chest and the years of childhood were over. She could never get it right and she had to do it over and over a million times to get this skirt with its innumerable pleats in the order in which her mother wanted. But the sense of order and procedure, which Mama taught her, has remained. She realises this whenever her temper manifests itself in an impulse to strike at somebody or something and she would pause and take a deep breath and begin to count until she got to ten. Mama always said: 'Remember, a deep breath, then: One...two...three...to ten before you decide. Just do it pleat-by-pleat, one after the other, singly and continuously as you have learned. And when you come to the end, don't forget to *decide*. That is the secret to dealing with temper and anxiety. Count yourself lucky because most people never have the chance to learn this and you can tell by the loads of stupid things they do.'

In the momentary panic caused by the alarm clock and the flow of anxiety that followed, she took a deep breath and started counting...one...two...three...until she got to ten and took another breath. Now she had to find the list, her list of ten tasks. She started towards her handbag on the floor beside her shoes. But it wasn't in there. Yes, it was under the pillow, it had to be. She remembered how she had carefully folded it and stuck it inside between the pillowcase and the pillow. Now she made for the bed, pausing for a fleeting glance at the mirror where she saw that her hair, which she had put in curlers, was still intact which meant she had had a relatively peaceful sleep. Since Kunle went away, she always slept on one side of the bed, leaving the other half as if reserved for him. But the nightmares always ensured that even though she never rolled over during the night she woke up all the time with her hair in a mess. Last night was therefore a lucky exception.

On the bed, under the pillow, she found the piece of paper, rumpled but legible in her trademark masculine calligraphy, which elicited curiosity and comment from those who saw it for the first time and tried to match the ugly squiggles with the young woman before them. Her first task had to do with the baby – the list specified every little item from the diapers to the toys. She picked out each one – pleat by pleat, remember – and put them carefully away in the kit she had bought especially for the purpose. This was fairly easy but then she made sure after doing all of this to double-check: she counted the number of items specified in the list and matched this with the number in the kit. Correct, pleat after pleat, she murmured in satisfaction before moving on to the second task which was getting his food warmed. She always did this pleat-by-pleat, pleat after pleat stuff first in humorous imitation of her mother and later in a half-serious recall of the lesson she'd learned from it.

Now she went about the other tasks in a meticulous and orderly fashion reminding herself of the importance of this day. She was taking the baby to see his father for the first time and she knew that it would be a heart-rending experience for both father and son. The son wondering what this strange man was doing speaking to them from behind a cage of iron bars and the father trying to kiss this son separated from him by the cold bars. She had envisioned this scene so often that it had become part of her subconscious. Kunle had insisted at first that she not bring the child, but she had broken down his defences by insisting that it was important for the boy to see the reality of oppression early in life and therefore know how to live as a man in the country. What better way to do this than to see his father in jail and carry this memory imprinted on his mind?

'No, you can't bring a child to this place. He will have nightmares afterwards.'

'Better for him to have them now and learn to live with them than encounter them later.'

'Look here Lollipop,' he pleaded. 'This is not a place for a child.'

'Yes Coconut, I agree. Don't you think I understand your concern?' She argued. 'But this is the time to learn.'

Over the years, he had become used to her habit of saying 'I agree with you' only to disagree.

'All right then let's for once agree without disagreeing at the same time,' he said and then he summoned all the husbandly authority he could bring to his voice. 'For the last time, don't bring him here and that's final.'

She couldn't help breaking into laughter and getting into the game at the same time.

'No, no, no, Coconut head, remember in this place I wear the pants!' She said in her best American accent, laying the stress on the pants.

'And I wear the trousers,' he responded involuntarily, clipping the words in an imitation English accent, before he realised that he had been drawn into the game. They both laughed, as they understood that this discussion wasn't to get them anywhere.

They way they argued and disputed about this visit, you would have thought that this boy was in his adolescence or that he knew what fatherhood meant or at the very least that he knew his own father. Which he didn't. It was this that started Lola on those picture-sound lessons, which the little boy had now learned by heart. Funny face ... then Da da. He had become quite used to the face and also came to love the repeated rhythms of the double syllables: Da da, Da da, the boy would sing; and, singly and continuously, the mother thought. It all blended well with her own childhood lesson: pleat after pleat, pleat by pleat. Whenever they played this game, she always wondered if she would be as good a mother to this boy as her mother had been to her, that woman of words who had filled her childhood with a diet of tales. She tried to lavish as much attention on him as she could; telling him stories to sleep, recounting the horrifying narrative of his father's arrest and spicing it with heroic deeds and colourful encounters, singing the songs her mother had taught to accompany the new episodes she invented.

*

When she arrived at the prison later that morning, she discovered that they had moved him to a new cell beside the lifers and the condemned. The guard led her through a labyrinthine series of stairs crawling with rodents. The dull light from the bulbs created so lugubrious an atmosphere she felt cold to the marrow. She was going through the most horrifying catacombs of hell, a place for demons to burn in. With the one hand she carried her baby balanced on her hip and with the other she tried to steady herself, to keep from falling by holding on to the railing. She didn't mind that it was oily, damp and sticky, she held on, taking one laboured step after the other, her nose twitching from the horrible smell pervading the entire prison.

'Are you all right?' The guard asked her, trying for all the world to appear compassionate and caring.

'Yes,' she replied, avoiding his eyes.

'Make I help you carry the pickin?' He offered.

'Thanks,' she answered, passing the kit over to him even though she understood that he had offered to help with the baby. The thought of giving her boy to him even for a little while was not one she could contemplate.

The guard dutifully took the kit and was mildly surprised that it was so heavy. He never stopped to wonder what it was that women logged around in their handbags that made them so heavy. Surely it couldn't just be lipsticks and make up. His own mother was the worst example. She would fill the handbag with odds and ends, and then stick stuff into her bra cups and everywhere else she could use as a cargo hold. And even then she still cut a stately figure walking down the street. And this woman was no different, climbing the prison stairs as if she were going into a palace.

What he didn't know was that Lola had carefully cultivated this attitude. On her first visit to the prison, she had looked so forlorn and depressed that Kunle was shocked on seeing the shell of a woman approaching him. The odour of defeat and despair on her was so pungent that he could smell it; he knew it from his association with the prisoners and could smell it from their sweat when they perspired and from their cells when they were asleep. It drifted to him whenever he met them along the corridors and exchanged brief pleasantries with them; gradually, he had become used to it emanating from their bodies. But, that day, when he looked into the visitors' lounge and the odour wafted towards him from his wife he was frightened. What could have happened to this woman whose infectious joy had turned his life around? The woman who read him poems and sang him songs on nights when the weight of work and the horrors of the journalist life sent him into bouts of depression? Surely, that was not the woman sitting down over there with that snivelling look of self-pity? He strode briskly to the cage as she came to him on the other side of the steel bars. He knew that he had to put up a front, to comfort her and assure her that it was all right, that it was only a matter of time before the dictator was overthrown and he would breathe the sweet scent of freedom once again.

When he stuck his lips through the bars to give her a kiss, he was all smiles. He told her how he was treated like a prince in a castle, how the guards begged him not to count this against them when he was released, how the prisoners wanted him to see to their own freedom when he became president of the country; how they took turns to wait on him at meal times, how he had been placed on a special diet and a thousand other lies by which he tried to put a favourable face on his circumstances.

'Now you come here looking like a pauper's wife,' he continued. 'What do you want them to think of me?'

For all his effort, he knew that she did not believe him. He switched tactics and turned the entire meeting into one long session of jokes.

'You have to go and change and make sure you come back here with immediate effect!'

She could no longer help herself and she burst into prolonged laughter. And that was how the entire day had proceeded form one joke to the other until she promised never to come visiting in those clothes again. From that day, she had kept her word every time she visited. She wore her best skirts and tops and when she wore her close-fitting trousers she made sure to emphasise the curves of her hips and the fullness of her bum, to highlight the sensuousness of her lips with a generous smear of lipstick, and to walk with a sassy girlish sway that was seductively inviting. She made some angry and jealous because she seemed to act as if prison was one big ball for her husband.

Today, the guard was only seeing one half of the persona she always donned; the half that wore the lovely clothes, the sassy steps were gone, driven away by the load of anxiety she carried to this visit. Although the boy had learned the Da-da-act perfectly, she still felt with a woman's intuition that something would go wrong today. And his relocation to another cell was only the first indication. She couldn't quite lay her finger on it but the feeling was so strong she could not ignore it. It was palpably there, knotted somewhere within her, tugging at her heartstrings from the security of its claw-hold in the interstices of her guts. But she continued, following behind the guard and wondering when this journey of agony would end.

Finally, after the interminable flight of stairs, they arrive. There are a few people in the visitor's lounge. Lola always dreaded this moment because she never wanted to find one of his friends also waiting to see him on the days she visited. The time was too short to be shared and today, being so special, it would be disastrous to have someone else there. That was why she had chosen the anonymity of a hotel, a place where she would not be recognised, away from curious friends. A quick look at the waiting faces and she was relieved. There was no one she recognised. The guard offered her a bench and carefully laid the kit on it. Kunle had already been contacted so he was bound to be on his way. She was about to put the baby down when a gaunt bearded man smiling from the first enclosure beckoned at her. She stared at him for a moment before recognising her husband behind the scraggy growth of beard, the sunken eyes and the emaciated skeletal look. She gasped in surprise at the picture and in a trice she realised what all her premonitions had been about. There was no way the son could recognise the father; the Daddy in the photograph had receded into a mask of skull and bones and beard.

Come on baby,' he said, stretching his hands through the bars.

She lifted the boy up and walked towards him.

'My God, what have they done to you?' She screamed before she realised what she was doing. She had no business being hysterical with the boy right there with her. She raised her handkerchief hand to her mouth and immediately began to count. 'One...two...three...pleat by pleat, pleat after pleat...' she reminded herself. 'Four...five...six...pleat after pleat, pleat by pleat...smoothen it with your hand...make sure it is properly folded...then place the iron on it...one pleat at a time, pleat by pleat, gently...seven...eight...nine...'

It wasn't working; this was like trying to stop an earthquake with bare hands. Trying to force the lid down on a boiling pot. She could feel the molten lava already choking her. She had to begin all over again...count one by one...pleat by pleat...

It isn't working! The panic rose, exploded through her throat into her mouth. Damn it O God! She was now by the bars; her hands were shaking so much she could hardly hold the baby but his hands were still sticking out. She thrust the baby into them and ran off with rocket speed to the ladies she had seen around the corner on their way in. There she threw up all her anger, all her sorrow and helplessness. She kept throwing up until she felt her guts would spill out. It seemed an eternity before she heard her baby's cry. The voice was coming from a distance and it ripped through the landscape of mists and haze in which she had been temporarily lost and found its way into her consciousness. Then carefully, very calmly, she wiped away her tears, pleat by pleat, washed her mouth, pleat after pleat, rinsed her face, one two three, and walked out, towards the sordid hall and that enclosure which held her husband.

Now she started reciting the poem they always shared when one of them was depressed or in pain.

> *Leave them alone, my love, leave them alone*
> *Forget the owls hooting away the night*

115

Forget the flood of blood on the streets
Let the claps of thunder and the rattle of rain
Bring you to me and for this one night
Come; walk through my door of dreams…

He never allowed her finish the poem because her always interrupted at this point to add his silly phrase.

And enter into my nightmares!

Now, she walked into the nightmare, strong and confident, as her mother would have wanted. She took the boy from his hand and he immediately stopped bawling. Then she brought out the photograph and pointing to it said, 'Da da.'

'Da da,' he repeated.

She turned the photo and pointed to the man in the enclosure and said once again: 'Da da.'

The boy waited and took a closer look, then shook his head so vehemently that even she was surprised.

'Yes, Da da,' she encouraged him trying to place him on the outstretched hands once again. But he started bawling all over again and clasped his mother firmly.

'This is Daddy, yes, go, go and say hello.' She tried to coax him by passing his favourite toy to his dad. Still he refused any contact and would not say the magic words. They were his and his mother's alone, not to be shared with this bearded stranger.

She kept trying; convinced that she would get the response she had spent so much time on. But the boy was resolute and the father had to ask her to stop.

Today, the boy seemed to be saying, there was not going to be any Da da, at least not here in front of this cage and certainly not before this bearded stranger.

It had become obvious to Kunle that the boy was not going to budge and that no decent conversation could take place with Lola today.

'I think you should take him home and come back alone in the evening.'

'I am sorry, Kunle.'

'Come on Lollipop, there is nothing to be sorry for. Can't you see that the little brat has inherited his father's stubborn will,' he said, laughing.

She knew that the laughter was forced, that he was only trying to put a good face on a disastrous visit but she accepted it and carefully began to gather her things together. She gave him a forced smile and said, 'See you later in the day. And meanwhile: eat. Here is something special for you.'

As they left, Kunle stared at them and for the first time, since the day of his arrest, he felt the asphyxiating constriction of confinement: the lively little bird in his chest for once refused to fly; it seemed to have suddenly lost its wings and fallen into the gloomy airless pit of death; it's song choked by the evil noises of chattering owls. He shuffled away from the enclosure praying that this bird not die, that it hibernate with him for the many years he remained in prison and, like a phoenix, rise again on resurrection morning and fly into the sunlight of freedom.

Lola left the jailhouse and walked into the sunlight thinking: 'Today, Da da failed, and pleated skirts failed.' But as she tried again to make sense of it all, the boy saw the look of sorrow on his mother's face and wanted to cheer her up. He started swaying and soon he was chanting that Da da Da da Da da that always lifted her from the marshes of sorrow. In shock and surprise, she turned to him murmuring her pleat after pleat, one two three, in unison.

That evening, she did not go to the prison. She spent the time sketching a new picture of Da da and as she drew the whole house was rocking with the boy's trilling rendition and her choral accompaniment.

JUDGEMENT A COME

By

May L. Quadri

The twenty women who had confessed to witchcraft thrashed and twitched on the ground as the man of God railed over their prostrated bodies, exhorting them to submit to his powers.

It was a great crusade in the town of Sapele, one of the many that the man of God had planned for various towns in the country, healing the sick and attacking the forces of evil.

The followers of the man of God looked on in awe, mixed with admiration, as he fervently prayed the evil forces in the witches to come out or be dealt with by the Holy Ghost. In true miraculous fashion, some of the women spewed out so much of their innards that the onlookers gasped in horror; scared that these women would die from agony. However, it seemed that they could not control whatever sensation they were going through. For many of the people at the revival, it was a great show watched with keen interest.

One of the witches whirled on the same spot like an agbegijo masquerade, feet barely touching the ground. Then, she screamed, raised her body up as if asking God to accept her and free her from the torture of the exorcism before descending to the ground with a loud crash. It was beyond the ordinary and somehow it was beyond the magical. After a while, she opened her mouth and vomited out blood and a thousand and one objects. Many would swear later that she vomited her intestines and some actually said she died, even though she was only unconscious, but those who were present found the fear of God branded permanently on their souls. Some said afterwards that it was the ultimate power of the Holy Ghost at work and many whose hearts had been hardened to God gave their lives in total submission. It was hard not to succumb under the circumstance.

> Judgement a come
> Nowhere to run
> No place to hide.

New converts flocked to the revivals of the man of God, seeking deliverance or finding a light and cause that made their previous lives seem like nothing compared to what now lay ahead of them. His became the biggest church in the land in a matter of months and rumours started flying right and left that he would appear at different towns around the country at the same time to preach. Once you beheld the power of this man of God, there was no doubting the possibility of the feat. There was even a rumour once or twice that he was not born of an association between a man and woman, but that his mother had been filled with the spirit. Anyway, she was dead now and could not be approached for corroboration.

Wealthy people contributed fortunes into his ministry to have an audience with him. At the close of every crusade, there was always a stampede as the crowd fought to touch him or at least the hem of his garment. Of course the wealthy who sat at the ring side seats got the real thing while the poor in the popular gallery often resigned themselves to the odd outstretch of hands. Even then, many swore they felt his touch from about fifty metres away.   His television programme, which he started out paying for, was moved to a prime time slot, for free, and blue chip companies scrambled over one another to gain the sponsorship. The ratings of his programme and its repeats were the highest in the land, to such an extent that it was noticeable in the city traffic; when the programme was on, the country virtually came to a standstill.

The ministry quickly organised a band that played to larger and larger crowds as the crusade crossed the country like a touring rock band, singing the song now accepted as the anthem of the crusade:

> Judgement a come
> Nowhere to run
> Nowhere to hide
>
> Judgement a come
> Who no know, he go know
> Who no *sabi*, he go *sabi*

The man of God put the fear of God in people, though some actually said the fear related more to him. Because of this, many of his followers started planning- secretly of course- to have him take on the military dictatorship and announce himself the next President of the country. You could almost hear the "let him be Caesar!" from his congregation. There was no limit to the veneration in which his followers held him.

The man of God however continued his work to rid the country of evil forces. In Otta, he had been threatened by the town elders not to hold his crusade during the Oro festival but the man of God would not be deterred. Despite threats to his followers, he ordered women especially to turn up in open defiance of the Oro worshippers. For those who believe in the Word, there is nothing to fear, he said, holding up the Bible. According to town sources however, those who turned up at the crusades did so because of their belief in the man of God and not the Word.

True to practice, the elders carried sacrifices to the venue every day of the crusade and each time the man of God joked that he would have eaten it if it did not looking so unappealing. A bit of nightlife remained in the town despite the warnings and threats, because so many people depended on the assurances of the man of God, an unlikely occurrence in the month of Oro. The heat was on and the whole of Otta knew they would never witness such a time ever again. Nobody had ever dared the council of elders and the potency of their *juju* before.

There were testimonies each night by women who had caught in the wake of Oro on their return home but lived to tell the tale against conventional wisdom. One of particular note was a woman who said she had been cornered by an Oro who was stark naked. Fiery looking men surrounded her chanting incantations. She was scared initially that they might rape or kill her and when she opened her mouth to scream, nothing came out. Then she remembered the preaching of the man of God. Immediately, as she began to pray, calling on God to deliver her, the strangest thing happened – a bolt of lighting struck the earth between her and the Oro and that was it. She saw the Oro going round and round in a circle looking for her but he couldn't find her, while she became invisible to him.

The following day, two of the Oro chiefs went blind. A meeting of the council of elders was immediately summoned, where the two blind elders insisted that the council took the most drastic measures to avenge this affront to their culture. One of them suggested spraying the man of God with the most potent pepper corns available for an instant cancerous growth to develop all over his body. As the volunteer carried the pot of the cancerous concoction towards the crusade ground, he suddenly turned the contents over himself, inflicting himself with immediate cancer and a sure death. But that was not all. At the same time, spores of the juju spread to the two blind chiefs and caused growths all over their bodies.

The news of the power of the man of God spread even farther than before, and with more rapidity. He became so popular that some other Christian ministers started applying to become part of his ministry. Other denominations saw their membership dwindle as the country seemingly moved towards a one-church State. Even the head of state who was a Muslim, took notice of the man of God and ordered his security unit to place him under constant surveillance.

By now some of the more ardent believers now called him The Prophet. In the true makeup of prophets he had a calling, a brief, he was doing works of wonder and the international media joined the corps that followed him about. European and American sceptics got together to reveal his tricks because as far as they were concerned he had a method and despite weeks of sleepless nights they could not reveal any tricks. Stories, testimonies and confessions came from all quarters, often with hard evidence, that some started to murmur the possibility of a Second Coming of the Messiah. Analysis drew parallel between his age and life and that of Christ, but on that note the man of God refused to comment. He just carried on with his works.

Finally, the man of God decided to hold a crusade in Ile-Ife, the citadel of Yoruba civilisation and the origin of the Yoruba people. Unlike Otta, no challenge or threat was directed at him. Ile-Ife was reputed more for its people's stubbornness and its leaders' wisdom. Though, Ile-Ife people were predominantly Christians, many more people from all over the country flocked to the town ahead of the crusade, looking for miracles, healing and deliverance from enemies. Some just wanted to be close to the man of God, to hear his preaching and watch him perform his miracles.

Maybe it was for more publicity that the man of God felt prompted to initiate another stunt, or the sense of duty in the true manifest of his calling – to eradicate all acts of idol worshipping – the man of God decided to remove the age-old staff of Oranmiyan, one of the symbols of the independence of the Yoruba race. "It's an evil that must be destroyed," he said. The announcement to remove the staff met with a lot of consternation but little resistance. Some elders of the town sent a warning to the man of God, that they were not opposed to his crusade, but they wanted him to respect their culture and religion. The man of God sent a reply that until they come to know and accept Christ as their Lord and saviour; their chosen religion deserved no respect.

Immediately a meeting of the council of Yoruba elders and kings was called. After much deliberation, the decision was to do nothing. After all, when the white man challenged the Yoruba culture and failed despite his technology and force of character, the Yorubas did the same thing – nothing. Everyone knew that the gods in Yorubaland watched over the staff.

By the date of the crusade, Ile-Ife could not contain the visitors, both the devout and the curious. People came from all over the world to watch the removal of the staff that had defied science. The people of Ile-Ife made money from the sales of food and souvenirs. Many even rented their rooms and land to many of the foreign media networks to build huge tents. Multinationals came in with sponsorship and publicity, giving away food, sleeping bags, flasks, free drinks (all bearing their logo). All the schools closed, since the students were no longer turning up anyway. Others made money recounting the history of Ile-Ife and the staff to the various media organisations present. It seemed one only needed to be an indigene of Ile-Ife to be an expert. Everybody wanted to be part of history.

The whole country remained glued to television tubes and radios, waiting for the miraculous to happen, once again. It had been predicted that the millennium would hold many unusual things and nobody doubted this was one of the most unusual of feats predicted.

On the opening night of the crusade, the milling crowd rendered the town impassable. The small town was bursting at its seams. After a while, the man of God arrived in style, in a helicopter donated gratuitously by a television company. He was wearing a cream and gold silk lace material with elaborate embroidery in gold on the front of its *agbada*. His jet-black wavy curls sparkled in the light as he mounted the podium that had been built especially to give him access to the staff. The crowd cheered wildly, some doing acrobatic displays in ecstasy. Calmly he waited behind his lectern to let the cheer subside before he spoke. He promised a miracle on the night, stating that the night belonged to him to do whatever he wanted with the staff of Oranmiyan.

He then proceeded to acknowledge the presence of some dignitaries who were seated round the podium. Almost all the State governors were there, and the head of state had duly sent his deputy to represent him at the momentous occasion. The man of God welcomed all these people to the greatest show of the millennium. However, since the majority of Yoruba statesmen and kings did not dignify the occasion with their presence, the man of God did not acknowledge them.

He then asked the crowd if they wanted to see history made right in their presence.

The crowd went wild with their response. The man of God laughed.

He wiped his sweating face and asked once more. "Are you going to leave this place tonight and tell the world about the power of God?" The crowd screamed in unison; "yeeesssss!"

The cameras followed him as he made his way to the staff. All eyes were glued to him, and those who were outside his immediate vicinity watched the events on the giant screens erected throughout the arena. Yet, there were different versions of what happened that night, but almost everybody agreed that it had started from behind them – only a few said it started from the base of the Oranmiyan staff itself. All however agreed that it happened so suddenly that the eyes could not follow it, shattering every light, camera and screen around the venue and plunging the town of Ile-Ife and its environs into absolute darkness.

Sango, coming in a bolt of lightning, struck the man of God in the head and split him into two the very moment his hands touched the staff of Oranmiyan – the gods had risen to the challenge. Then molten lava filled the night, even though there were no volcanoes, dead or alive, in the vicinity of Ile-Ife, raining fires that burnt many and left scars that will remind them of the events of the day. Ile-Ife would remain silent for many weeks. The shock of the incident caused many to lose the use of their tongues for days. Not even the Yoruba elders could gloat at what clearly was their victory. The band remained silent and could not sing their anthem:

> Judgement a come
> Nowhere to run
> Nowhere to hide.

GAS AND BLOOD.

By

Ganja Ekeh

> "Bangigbe na goat-io, na goat-io.
> Bangigbe na goat-io! Omo eran!"

> "Bangigbe? Ole! Bangigbe? Thief!"

> "Aya e e e aya!
> Aya e e e aya! Aya we don come o,
> aya,
> pata pata we go win today o,
> aya!"

> "We no go gri o we no go gri,
> eeee trouble we no go gri."

> "ALL WE ARE SAAAAYING,
> GIVE US WATER!"

That last chant just didn't seem to coincide with our requests for General Bangigbe and his wife to quit government. Yet there seemed no more a suitable line to put but "give us water" at that section. The student union leader got on his megaphone and addressed the crowd.

"Greateeeeeeeest U-ites!"

"Greaaat!" we responded.

"Greateeeeeeeeeeeeeest U-ites!"

"Greaaat!"

He held his right hand up in the black power signal popularised in Nigeria by Fela Anikulakpo Kuti. The megaphone wasn't functioning as it should, and from my vantage point I couldn't really pick out what he was saying:

"Resident -an-gbe has defused to <buzz> <buzz> <crackle> criminal!"

The students roared their agreement in one loud shout. I roared too. Didn't care what he was saying, as long as this riot meant school would be closed and I wouldn't have to take my exams (which were just two weeks away). I can't say it was all my fault
that I was not ready. I mean, with lecturers like Mr. Abiku who said things like: "If I cash di student who is chooking my daughtah, I wi' ki' dem. And if you tink
dat you are all going to pazz dis khos witout 'aving brain of genius, den you are a mistake."

Mr. Abiku was a wicked man; of that there was no doubt. But when his daughter became pregnant he flipped. He actually went crazy. The university should have done something about it as soon as it happened. He was stark, raving mad.

Just the other day we saw Mr. Abiku at FLT. FLT was our affectionate name for the Faculty Lecture Theatre-a large but spooky theatre which doubled as a lecture hall by day, and a harem by night. I was strolling back to the main campus with my girlfriend, Sherrifat, when we saw Mr. Abiku running by the lakeside behind FLT. He had on a cape, not unlike Superman's, and he was singing in unknown tongues. Sherri and I immediately hid, for we were not sure what to make of it. It was a good thing we did, for Mr. Abiku abruptly picked up a stick and proceeded to brutally flog a couple who were hidden (or so they thought) in a corner.

"Is pipul like you! Is pipul like you! I wi' ki' you today!" he screamed at the top of his lungs while the stick rose and landed several times a second. The male member of this duo, once he had gathered his wits about him, found it convenient to push the female against

Mr. Abiku and run away-rather naked. I later found out that as he ran past Sultan Bello Hall, without realizing he was without apparel, a mob of students assumed he was a thief and chased him till he was caught. He took a severe beating that night, I understand, and when

they found out that he wasn't a thief, all he got was "sorry."

Sherri and I didn't wait to see what Mr. Abiku would do next before we decided that it was time for our own evening jog. We tore back to campus in a hurry as the girl's screams resoundingly echoed. I had always thought that in a situation like that I would be like

Bond-James Bond. "Unhand the maiden!" I would shout, whereupon the villain would turn around and face me. 'Gen gen gen gen', the music would roar in the background and I would use my pen as a gun, my collar as a bullet shield, and my wit as my backup. So why did I then find myself half-shouting, "The Lord is my shepherd. I shall not want! I even went as

far as trying to speak Latin, as Father Munoz the Catholic priest used to. With Sherri and I breaking the sound barrier, I started my Gregorian chant. Ladies and gentlemen, the Apostle's Creed:

"Credo imu mu tetteh! Ago domino o teteh!"

I think it was more Urhobo and Yoruba than Latin, but God would understand.

Chants of "Shikin pie! Shikin pie!" brought me back to reality. Around me it seemed the students had come to some sort of decision. Apparently the student Government felt that one of the ways in which to force General Bangigbe to return all the money he and his wife had stored in Swiss banks, as documented by the pamphlets we all had, were to go to the University Staff Club and pillage, carting away as much "Shikin pie" and Pepsi as we could. True, things were not the same at The Staff Club. The chicken pies contained more boiled yam than they did chicken, and the swimming pool was being used as a case study on amoeba. But it was free food nonetheless, and the rationale was simply that if the General could siphon the goodies of our oil money using his power, then we could do ours through rioting.

As the elders once said, "*awoof no dey run belle.*" I followed the crowd as the leaders led the way from the Student Union Building, past Mellanby Hall, the bookstore, and behind the Catholic church. It was there that Pius Ezikwe, the altar boy, surprised father Munoz by leaving confession to join the people in their struggle-the great shikin pie revolution. Finally we got to the Staff Club. A few people were a bit annoyed because no one would allow them to break into the Catholic Church and take the Holy Communion. They apparently thought it had magical properties which could cure hunger for long periods of time, and was also apparently very tasty, judging by the way Father Munoz always wolfed down seventeen or so when he was doing the pre-communion prayer. This always pissed me off because there would only be half a communion wafer for each congregation member, after Munoz had munched half of the communion and drank most of the wine. Maybe the man was hungry, but such were the benefits of priesthood.

Less than an hour later, we had accomplished our duties and looted the University Staff Club. There was even roasted chicken kindly donated to us by our hosts. Our rendezvous certainly made up for the many nights I spent eating eba with the aroma of soup. That's right, Oppress (my roommate) and I would make eba and stand outside the door of our neighbours. We would then place the eba in the path of the smell of the soup-and then eat it. Times were hard. Oh, but how about when we finally had money to make rice, ehn? I say how about those times? I say, the VERY moment the rice was done, having mixed it with a concoction of eggs, whatever meat we could find, and several leaves, which Oppress claimed, would fill us till Tuesday, six or seven of our closest friends would suddenly appear for a visit (brandishing spoons-as you normally do would when visiting someone). Ah, these people. Toyota. Bobo, Patto. Akpoko-jones. Cincinatti and Tarantula. These folks did not mess around when it came to that rice, o. And these people, did they have coolers in their mouths or what? They would just expertly use the back of the spoons to flatten their portion of the pot, "shmeh, shmeh," and then deposit it, burning hot as it was, in their mouth. "Phhh! Phh!" They would blow twice, and then their spoons were in the pot again. Those times were hard I say.

I licked my fingers as we made our way towards the university main gate. There, as was the practice, we would barricade it, burn a couple of cars, and sing songs of war. I felt like sleeping. I burped. That chicken was good sha. I had been surprised to see many employees of the Staff Club assist us in looting. Yet while we malnourished students focused on the food, they seemed more interested in something else as I could constantly hear the cash register ringing. I guess it was bonus time.

We got to the gate and the war began. We transformed a couple of *Danfo* buses into firewood and began to sing and dance. This was the typical riot practice for students. I used this opportunity to get to meet Lara. Ah, sexy Lara. Her friends called her "Lawa" because she couldn't pronounce the letter "r," but used "w" instead. Apart from that, she was flawless. She really did look like Joy-girl, but even better. I knew she'd just broken up with her boyfriend (an ingrate who mistreated this specimen of beauty) and she was lonely. You know, a consoling shoulder was just what she needed. I'd always liked Lara but never had the opportunity to meet her. True, I had a girl, but a little indiscretion never harmed anyone. Right, Monica? And I knew she wanted to meet me too, but my girl Sherrifat was in most of my classes so there was no escape. But Sherri, pretty and proper, was not the rioting type-Lara was. She was my type of woman. Or she would be till such indiscretions jeopardized my relationship with Sherri. This was just the way of the world at the time. It was the protocol, the way things were done. Everyone understood this. I got into my comedian mode, having been tutored by the venerable comedian Sele Anini.

"These people no sabi entin!" I boasted, as Lara looked on with her friends laughing. "You see this scar here? This was from Stadium when I finish the Alector Brodas. If you see dem, ask dem about me? They will tell you my story!" Lara was enjoying herself, holding a stick, with her jeans ripped in several places revealing more than a fair share of smooth skin. She knew what was up. Within the course of twenty minutes Lara and I had started talking and I was using "style-style" to get closer. You know about "style-style" don't you? I know you know about "style-style".

Style-style is when you laugh, and use the laughter to carry your body to lean on the girl. You get. Anyway, since I didn't get any negative vibes from her, (in fact she was also using the method to place her hands on my laps) I continued and soon we were sitting down, with my head against her chest as we spoke. It felt so natural. It felt so natural. My head rose and subsided as her breathing pushed her breasts up and down. She was so loving and soft. What a woman.

"So where is that your girlfriend, Shewi?" She asked. "Oh, well, we kind of broke up for a while" I lied. "Hmm! Super G! You think I'm one of your *I.S.I* girls? Who do you think you're telling this kin' stowy? You Silly wat!"

We laughed long and hard. I was ecstatic. Lara, or "Lawa" as I now called her, was known as a "senior girl" on campus, but we won't discuss that now for suddenly there was a stampede. It sounded like a billion elephants running.

I tried to get up quickly, trying to figure out what was going on, but people kept inadvertently kicking me back to the ground as they ran. I heard several loud bangs and the air suddenly turned white and red. Clouds of teargas surrounded me and I could hardly make out where I was. I immediately removed my shirt and applied some kerosene to it from the little "Jeri can" I had carried. I put the shirt to my nose and began to feel my way around, looking for Lara. Many of the students had run to safety by that time, and as the smoke cleared I thought I could see the figures of anti-riot policemen advancing. I stumbled upon Lara. She was on the floor choking. I pulled her up with all my strength and tried to drag her, moving as fast as I could away from where I thought I saw police. Lara was coughing severely, and the effect of the kerosene on my nose was dying down. As though out of intuition I turned around briefly and what I saw scared me. It wasn't policemen I had seen the first time. I had seen soldiers.

I had seen soldiers.

I knew then that I was going to die.

The smoke had cleared enough for me to make out a line of soldiers with rifles pointing in our direction. I closed my eyes and waited to die. BLAM! BLAM! BLAM! BLAM! Several shots rang out and I felt a force push me to the ground. I lay there for at least an hour, not moving, and trying not to breath heavily. There was something on top of me, but I didn't know what it was. Gunshots rang out all the while and I heard screams everywhere. I lay still.

I must have passed out for I was awoken by a group of students around me trying to talk to me. "He's alive! Thank God!" I heard someone say. I focused and saw a group of people sprinkling water on my head. I placed my hands to my forehead and felt a liquid. It wasn't water. I looked at my hands-red. I looked down at my body-red. But I didn't feel any pain. I turned on my side and felt massive stabs of pain.

And there she was: Lara lay there covered all over with blood-her blood, her life. I was too shocked to do anything. I tried to speak but no words came out. She was still breathing.

Her eyes opened slowly and focused on me. She summoned up what seemed like an inordinate amount of strength and managed a genuine smile. She looked so beautiful.

So innocent.

So beautiful. "Shhhhhh..." I tried to tell her to conserve energy by not speaking, but her eyes defied me.

"You silly wat" she whispered, and then smiled again. She was so beautiful. "I'll tell Shewi."

I was crying but there were no tears. Lara died seconds later. I closed my eyes and tried to wake up. When I opened my eyes again all I saw was a lost life, teargas canisters, and a pool of blood.

Nigerian youth died that day.

I MUST KILL SQUINTY

By

Chukwuma Okoye-Nwajeiaga

The very many injuries of Squinty I have borne, like the patient long-suffering gentleman that I am. But, come on, there is a limit to what a man can bear. When things get to a head, when a man's back is to the wall, then a man's gotta do what a man's gotta do. I've had it up to here from Squinty so there's no more room in my long-suffering heart to condone, forgive, or forget. I am bent on vengeance: I MUST KILL SQUINTY. For my peace of mind, self-respect and sanity, I must eliminate Squinty. Call me what you will – murderer, sadist, whatever – my mind is made up. I HAVE TO DO IT.

Now imagine this: Not once in weeks – nay, months – has my wife said to me "Oh darling" affectionately. She never does. Not even on those special occasions. Occasions, which have become even more occasional. All she says is "oh, ah Boy!" in variable pitches and accents. But never "oh darling" affectionately. Never affectionately. Of course she calls me "darling" with alarming regularity. When she sends me on errands. Then adopting several effeminate gestures – you know, flicking the head from side to side, rolling the eyes, fluttering the lashes, flicking the wrist and so on – she would say "oh darling could you make me a cup of coffee, please". Then she would be sitting on the couch reading glamour magazines with her slim attractive legs crossed, displaying beautifully manicured nails.

"Will you be a sweetie and pass me my dressing gown." Yes, she somehow always manages to go into the bathroom without her dressing gown. She delicately slips out of it, allowing it to flutter gracefully to the bedroom floor, then steps over it and bounces her nakedness into the bathroom.

"Oh darling could you run down the stairs and fetch my handbag from my car." You wouldn't believe she'd only just walked in. She always does that. She always leaves her handbag behind. Perhaps she believes that a light weight is dangerous to her model frame. Sometimes I do sincerely believe that she is determined to kill me in matrimony. Not with any of those things a married man silently vows to be killed with. But with errands. "Oh darling" or "Sweetie" from her is anything but sweet. It is hell. She never says it affectionately. Never to me. To Squinty, yes, but never to her long-suffering husband.

Now let me tell you a little about Squinty. Whenever my wife comes back from wherever, she ascends the stairs, her arms spread out expectantly as Squinty bounces down. Midway she would pick him up with "Oh darling did you miss me?" "Oh darling it's all right now I'm here." "Oh darling did you eat well?" Oh sweetheart I missed you." And the impudent, uppity Squinty would snuggle into her arms, whimpering and whining, wriggling his body like mosquito lava. And sometimes while all this emotion is being expressed, I stand behind her, forlorn and patiently suffering. I never complain... aloud. In fact, I have an unbeaten record in that feat. So there I would stand on the stairs, behind my wife, as she cuddles a whimpering, whining, and wriggling, silly, impudent and uppity Squinty. One eternity later both would end up on the couch, with his head in my wife's lap, his right eye closed while he tries to monitor my jealousy with the left. "Oh darling you must be hungry." To Squinty of course-affectionately.

"Oh darling could you run down the stairs and fetch my handbag from my car." Make no mistake about it; that is to me. So off I go down the stairs, wondering for the umpteenth time why she always seemed to put emphasis on "My car" without actually seeming to... I sometimes think I imagine it. But it is always there. It is not as if I have ever made the mistake of thinking the car is mine or ours. Of course it's her car. It's always been her car. It is a wedding present from her parents. So I open the door to her white Volkswagen Santana and retrieve her bag wedged between the two upholstered front seats. As I ascend the stairs two at a time I wonder why I banged the door a little too hard. Not anger. I simply cannot be angry. I'm incapable of that. Not jealousy either, perhaps I simply imagined it – that I banged the door a little too hard, that is. As I step into the room I notice a sneering expression on Squinty's face. Now I certainly did not imagine that. It's there in white and brown – the white around the left eye and the brown of the lips. I know a sneer when I see one. "Here you are," I say as I hand the handbag to my wife. "Oh thank you. Ehm, darling, could you please get me a glass of water from the fridge." So to the refrigerator I go and return with a glass of water. "Here you are," I say as I hand over the glass of water to my wife. "Oh thank you," she says.

And then I see that sneer again. So I make a wicked face at Squinty as my wife settles down to the delicate and graceful art of sipping water from a narrow glass without generously smearing the edge of the glass in the disgusting pink of her lipstick. (No matter how delicately she does it she never succeeds.) Soon the silly, impudent and uppity Squinty whines in protest. "Oh darling what is it?" my wife enquires. Fortunately God made sure his silly impudence has no way of articulating any words of English. "Are you hungry?" "Ugh" Squinty grunts. "Sweetheart, just a minute." To Squinty, of course. She heads for the refrigerator. She actually believes he said "yes". But then Squinty has never refused a quart of milk from the refrigerator so there really is no way of knowing if he said "yea" or "nay".

So here I sit on the couch opposite Squinty. I take a look at his smiling insolence and renew my vow: "I MUST KILL SQUINTY! For my peace of mind, self respect and sanity, I must eliminate Squinty." Right there and then I begin the search for a way. I certainly cannot bring myself to literally chop off his head like an *Ogun* sacrifice. I am not that barbaric.... There must be a civilised way. I have it! I am going to make of him a sacrifice to Ogun after all, but in a less barbaric manner. I shall rake him to the highway and abandon him there. There, an unwary driver will inevitably run him down. Simple and neat. All I need do is wait for about an hour until my wife locks herself in for her inevitable two hours beauty siesta. Then Squinty, we shall find out who will have the last sneer. Silly impudent and uppity mongrel. Of course Squinty, you are nothing but a mongrel. My wife would kill me if she hears me call you that. She says you are a certain breed – I can't remember what foreign-sounding word she uses. But every hated dog is a mongrel. To her you can be anything else. But to me you are a bloody mongrel, Squinty. Mongrel! You can sneer all you wish. We'll see who will have the last sneer. Bloody mongrel!

Squinty leaps off the couch and rushes to the disgustingly obscene business of lapping a quart of milk all up in twenty seconds. Go on Squinty, you are doing your last lap. "Oh darling I'm off to siesta" I almost respond in error to what is meant for Squinty. Squinty looks up at my wife and says something like "I'm going to miss you", and then executes a last lap. Lucky for me my wife never admits any form of disturbance to her beauty siesta. While she sleeps the country could stop, wait or simply disintegrate for all she cares. So Squinty, she can't take you with her. It's going to be your sneering insolence and my wronged self. Squinty walks her halfway to her bedroom door and then leaps unto the couch as she disappears. I watch Squinty as he settles himself on the couch, supporting his long, fat head gracefully with his crossed forelimbs as he demurely and luxuriantly closes his eyes. But I know Squinty. He wants me to believe he is sleeping. But I know better. He is waiting for me to go into my own bedroom so he can go and lie down before my wife's bedroom door. But there you are wrong Squinty. All I have to do is wait for another five minutes and I'm sure my wife won't hear the sound of her car engine as I take you out on a trip down Ogun's gluttonous throat. Just you wait and see. Time up. So I get up gently. There. I told you Squinty is not asleep. He opens his left eye slightly and spies on me. "Squinty," I whisper. He opens both eyes, puzzled by this unprecedented display of familiarity.

"Come on darling, let's go for a drive" 'darling' indeed. Squinty squints quizzically and snorts in puzzlement. I pick up the puzzled, quizzical, squinting, Squinty; I pick up the bunch of keys which has my wife's Volkswagen Santana car keys in it, and head for the stairs that would inevitably lead us to Ogun's altar. The silly, impudent and uppity mongrel begins to protest, but to no avail. I take the stairs three at a time. By the time my wife wakes up two hours from hence I would be back, and in my own room, savouring the gleeful taste of vengeance. Then the only "oh darling" addressee would be me, affectionately or otherwise, the former the better. If she asks for his whereabouts I would simply say, "Go look in the Boys' Quarters". And that would be it. She would look and would not find. His sneering impudence would have been left behind, awaiting Ogun's appetite.

So into the backseat I throw Squinty and off I drive, highway-wards. I hit the highway in less than two minutes but I drive on. Determined to take Squinty as far as possible. I hear they rarely lose their way because of their strong sense of smell. And that they often mark their track by pissing occasionally along the road as they go. Well, Squinty, there's no piss marking for you and– I wind up all the windows now, to be sure – there's going to be no detective smelling for you. Ogun, here comes thy sacrifice. I stop after six kilometres. I consider that a most appropriate distance. Surely there's no way this squinting arrogance can find his way back. I park by the side of the road; open the door; step out of the car; open the back door; pick up the protesting Squinty; close the back door; and then put Squinty on the ground. He begins to wag his tail. I wonder why he is doing that. I thought they did that when they were happy. Definitely Squinty must have mistaken the situation. I cannot resist giving it a valedictory scratch on the skull. Then I almost begin to feel sorry for him. But when I remember the numerous injuries of Squinty that I have borne I cut out all emotion. So I get into the car. Squinty looks at me quizzically. Then he sits down and mutters something. From the look on his face I surmise he must have uttered something like "You dare not!" Well Squinty, I dare. Goodbye my impudent mongrel. As from now on there will be no more "Oh darling for you". I shut the door and start the engine. Squinty still sits, daring me with his face. I engage the gear and make a 'U - turn'. Squinty still sits, daring me with his sneer. I feel slightly uncomfortable. I expect the bloody mongrel to feel sad or whatever they feel when they are abandoned. Well it's his business really. Who cares about his feelings anyway? If I did we wouldn't be here in the first place, would we? He certainly never bothered about my own feelings when he relished the comfort of my wife's lap and sneered at me. He usurped my position as husband, so why should I waste my emotion on him? So I drive off very slowly. I look back just in time to see Squinty get up and begin to give chase. I smile. Does he expect to catch up with my wife's Santana? I smile again as I press hard on the gas pedal. I look back and see Squinty giving up. He is now simply strolling. I look back again and he is gone. I have left him behind. Good riddance to his insolence. It is just a matter of time until somebody would run him over and send him to Ogun. I feel much better now, so I turn on the stereo set. I usually do that first thing when I get into the car beside my wife. It's amazing how I totally forgot about it until now. I've been unduly pre-occupied with Squinty. I sway my head in time to the music. I notice that the sky seems to be getting dark. Perhaps it's going to rain. That would be nice. Then I shall enjoy a cool siesta.

All of a sudden the car begins to swerve towards the right. I wrestle it safely to the side and park. Flat tyre I suspect. I get out and look. The right front tyre is almost totally flat. I swear at it. I hate changing tyres. There's no way I do it without coming away with dirty palms and cuffs. Well, dirty palms and cuffs or not, I have to hurry up and do what I have to do or else I'll get soaked by the impending rain. I walk to the boot, open it and bring out the jack and the wheel spanner. I take both to the bad tyre and begin to go through the dirty business of turning the nuts and positioning the jack under the car. All of a sudden I hear a rumble in the sky, and before I can look up I feel a few quick drops of water on my back. I hasten with the jack. The drops of water multiply. I become more frantic. The drops become more determined. The spanner becomes slippery. I'm nearly soaked. The drops now turn into a heavy downpour. I give up and run into the car for cover. I'll continue with that business when the rain subsides. I cannot say exactly how long I spent waiting for the blasted rain to subside. But it was long. I fretted; sweated; nearly suffocated. I thought of my wife who must be on the last ten minutes of her beauty siesta. And then the rain stops abruptly. Now I get out to continue with the slippery and dirtier business of changing the flat tyre. Five and a half minutes later I'm back on the road, angry and nervous. Now what do I tell my wife when I get home? How am I going to explain where I've been, what if she suspects I'll be undone. Then I notice that the music is still playing. I turn it off angrily. There's certainly nothing to feel musical about. I drive on splashing into heavy puddles of water in my nervousness. I swear and curse endlessly. Finally I park the car in the garage. Then I take the stairs three at a time. As I turn the handle and put my right foot into the sitting room I hear my wife say "Oh darling you are wet" affectionately. I smile as I prepare to tell the lie about forgetting to turn off the air conditioner in the office and having to forgo my siesta and rush back to the office to turn it off. I stand in surprise. My mouth wide open. Alas! The affectionate "Oh darling" was not for me. Lying on her lap all wrapped up in my very own blanket is Squinty. And there is that unmistakable sneer. My wife looks up at me. "What's the matter?" "Nothing" I blurt out quickly. Then I walk into the sitting room. "Where did you go to that you left the front door open for Squinty to go and get himself wet?" "I had to rush to the office...." "Oh darling you'll soon dry up. I'll fetch my hair dryer." She gets up and walks into her room. I swear at Squinty but he simply sneers. Behold! He has the last sneer. But we shall see about that. I storm angrily into my bedroom. We shall see about that!

GLOSSARY

Agbada – A voluminous, embroidered dress worn by men, especially among the Yorubas of Nigeria

Agbegijo – An acrobatic masquerade (*Egungun*) reputed for dancing with heavy stacks of wood on the head.

Akara – Fried bean balls

Ashewo – Prostitute

Awoof no dey run belle – Popular Nigerian sarcastic saying meaning free food doesn't cause stomach upset.

Beast – Mercedes Benz 500 SEL

Beast ko, Monster ni – Not a beast but a monster. A play on the trade name of an expensive Mercedes Benz 500 SEL.

Chei – An Igbo exclamation, usually for regret.

Dabaru – Scatter

Danfo – A VW 10 passenger bus. One of the most popular forms of road transportation.

Dodo – Fried plantain, for food

Egungun – A masked dancer or masquerade

Eko – Soft pap made from maizemeal

Garri – The processed root of the Cassava plant. It is a staple food amongst Nigerians.

Godo-godo don jam GOC, all of dem com' scatter for road, com' begin hala – The Mobile Police contingent has collided with the GOC (General Officer Commanding)'s entourage and trouble has begun.

IBB – Ibrahim Badamosi Babangida. 'Evil genius' and former Nigerian military dictator.

ISI – International School Ibadan.

Jollof rice – Rice mixed with stew, common among the Wollof of the Gambia

Kaya – a person or group of persons who carry loads in marketplaces for money

Magun - A type of curse placed on a woman so that any man who has a sexual intercourse with her would reap the full implication of the curse, which, in most cases, is death.

Moin-moin – Steamed bean flour, a delicacy

Mopol – Mobile Police

Ogi – Ground maize prepared for meal

Ogun – Patron god of iron in the Yoruba mythology. The sacrificial animal for Ogun is dog.

Ole – Thief

Oloriburuku - Somebody with a bad fate

Olosi - Never-do-well

Oranmiyan – The grandson of Oduduwa, the acknowledged founder of the Yoruba race

Oro – The mask of a secret cult that is not supposed to be viewed by women

Oyinbo – White-skinned person or a westerner

Pickin – **Pidgin** English meaning -Child

Sabi – To understand – get an understanding of a situation.

Sango – The Yoruba patron god of Lightening, thunder and fire. Sango is reputed for his destructive power.

Shaba – A skirt with long slit worn by West African women

Tokunbo – From overseas: name usually given to persons or property acquired from outside Nigeria. More recently, name used for all used products imported from Europe.

UCH –University College Hospital.

Won ti Pa wa – They have killed us

About The Writers

Chukwuma Okoye-Nwajiaga–Writer, producer, Choreographer and teacher. Chuks teaches design and Make-up at the department of Theatre Arts, University of Ibadan, Nigeria. His play, *We The Beast* won the 1990 ANA (Association of Nigerian Authors) award. He has written, produced and choreographed several plays, screenplays and dances.

Sola Adeyemi – Completing his doctoral Thesis in Drama at the North Western University in the Republic of South Africa, Sola is an accomplished writer and critic. He is also a proficient theatre artist with many production credits in Africa. He currently works as the Website Editor of the Natal Witness, a South African regional newspaper. He also edited this collection of Short Stories.

Ganja Ekeh – Born OghenevboGaga Ekeh in Zaria, Northern Nigeria, Ganja attended the International School Ibadan and then, the University of Ibadan for about a year before enrolling at the State University of NY at Buffalo and studied Electrical Engineering. It was there that social experiences led Ganja to adopt a pseudo-revolutionary point of view, and the metaphoric name "Ganja." - to indicate a "high" state of mind. Presently he is engaged as an Electrical Engineer, " to pay the bills," while vigorously pursuing a creative lifestyle. Ganja has published stories on the Internet and is currently working on several projects including a play, a music album and a couple of books.

Kolapo Oyefeso (1960-1999) – Trained as a Pharmacist. He was educated at Government College, Ibadan and the University of Ife (now Obafemi Awolowo University). He started writing full time in 1990 leaving behind, a career as a Pharmacist. He wrote several poems, plays, and stories. *The Race*, his first children's story won the ANA award in 1996. Two volumes of his collection of poems and several children's stories are awaiting publication. He died after a brief illness in 1999

Sola Osofisan – A stubbornly proud Nigerian writer and performing artist resident in New Jersey, USA. He has strings of published works in various genres to his credit. He has also won the prestigious ANA awards for Poetry and Fiction. He currently edits his pet project – The Who is Who of Nigerians in America. His website www.nigeriansinamerica.com remains a major force in the documentation of the achievement of Nigerians in the USA.

Wale Okediran – Wale trained at the University of Ife (now Obafemi Awolowo University) as a Medical Doctor. He has published novels, short stories and poems including **Rainbows are for Lovers**, **After the Flood** and **Call to worship**. He has also won national and international awards for his writings. He is the Medical Director of Cornerstone Medical Centre in Ibadan, Nigeria.

Harry Garuba – Poet and critic. Formerly of the University of Ibadan, Nigeria, now a senior lecturer in English at the University of Zululand, South Africa. He has written several poems, stories and essays. He is one of the most respected younger generation literary critics and creative writing teachers in Africa.

May L. Quadri – A Nigerian writer and performer who has worked within the Nigerian and British theatres, electronic and print media, variously as actor, musician, columnist, correspondent and sub-editor. He has had short stories, articles and poems published. He his currently working on a major TV drama and a documentary film

Dear Friend,

Thank you for reading our collection of enjoyable stories. I am sure that you have found them riveting. Now, it is not enough to read this book without letting someone else enjoy it. If you would like to give this book, or any other on our list, as a gift, or you would simply like to buy a copy for yourself, fill out the coupon below and mail it to:

Smart Image
Direct Mail Dept.
12 Collinson Court
Great Suffolk Street
London SE1 1NZ
UK

Once we receive your payment, we will send the book of your choice to you within 10 days. Or visit our website at www.smartimage.org.uk.

Thank you,
The Publisher

....

Please rush................ copy/copies of.......................
....
To me (or to)......................................Mr/Mrs/Ms
Address...

....
....
....
I have enclosed a cheque for the sum of £...................
made payable to **Smart Image Enterprises.**

1 copy	£7:98p(inc. p&p)
2 copies	£15:00(inc. p&p)
10 copies	£65:00(inc. p&p)